Two Solo Together

I0543966

Kesorn Weaver

Two Solo Together

Kesorn Weaver

Pechrach Publishing
United Kingdom

Two Solo Together
By Dr Kesorn Pechrach Weaver
ISBN 978-1-912957-10-1
PECHRACH PUBLISHING
7 Boundary Road, Bishops Stortford, Hertfordshire, CM23 5LE, England, United Kingdom. Tel: (+44) 1279 508020
Published 2025 by Pechrach Publishing
Copyright © 2025 Kesorn Pechrach Weaver and Pechrach Publishing

Cover illustrations © Dr Kesorn Pechrach Weaver

This book is dedicated to

All Solo Friends

This book celebrates the beauty of connection at any age, the magic of Norway's winter skies, and the unexpected wonder of a journey that becomes so much more.

Message from the Authour

This book is inspired by my real-life experience aboard the *Ship*, an Ambassador Cruise Line ship, during the *Northern Lights* voyage from 1st November 2024 to 15th November 2024. It was a journey that opened up a new world for me—filled with unexpected friendships, fresh perspectives, and unforgettable memories. I felt compelled to share that experience with you.

As a solo traveller, setting off alone can sometimes feel daunting. But when solo travellers cross paths and choose to walk the same deck for a while, the journey becomes lighter, brighter, and so much more enjoyable. Many of my fellow solo friends, who knew me as an academic and technical writer, asked why I hadn't yet written a fiction novel.

I hope this book brings joy, inspiration, and perhaps a smile to every reader—especially solo travellers and cruise lovers—who understand the magic of meeting strangers and leaving as friends, somewhere out at sea.

Kesorn Weaver

22nd May 2025

Bishops Stortford, UK

Acknowledgments

I would like to extend my heartfelt thanks to all my wonderful Solo Friends who made this unforgettable journey so special. Your companionship, laughter, and shared adventures filled each moment with joy and meaning.

To **John Lewis**, thank you for your stories, your easygoing charm, and your warm, welcoming nature. You always brought a smile to our table and reminded us of the beauty of simply being present.

To **Lynda Yandell**, your kindness, thoughtful conversations, and gracious spirit turned ordinary moments into memorable ones. You were a true light on this voyage, and your support never went unnoticed.

To **Annie Behan**, your lively wit, energy, and sense of fun added sparkle to every day. From spontaneous chats to shared laughter over cake and coffee, you made even rainy days feel bright.

Each of you helped make this journey more than a cruise—you made it a story worth telling. Thank you for the memories, the friendship, and the inspiration.

Foreword

By Kesorn

This story began with a simple idea: what happens when two strangers set out alone on the same voyage, unaware that the waves will carry them not just to faraway ports, but closer to each other?

Solo Together was inspired by the quiet bravery of those who travel solo—not in search of someone, but in search of something: peace, adventure, renewal. It's about the unexpected moments that unfold when you're free from routine, surrounded by strangers who, like you, have chosen a path less predictable.

Samatha and Sean could have passed each other by. Two names on a passenger list. Two solo travellers with separate lives. But something changed when their paths crossed on a northbound cruise to Norway. What follows is a journey filled with laughter, late-night shows, meaningful glances, missed laundry pickups, and an undeniable connection that deepens as the days go on.

This story is a tribute to new beginnings at any age, friendships that form over coffee or cake, and the magic that lives somewhere between the ship's departure horn and the final call to disembark.

I hope you enjoy sailing with Samatha and Sean as much as I enjoyed following their journey. And perhaps, like them, you'll be reminded that the sea is full of surprises—and so is life.

Foreword

By Samatha

When I first booked the cruise, I wasn't searching for love. In truth, I wasn't even looking for company. I needed a break—a reset—a chance to see new places and breathe new air. Travelling solo was something I had always wanted to try. It sounded brave. A little scary. And exactly what I needed.

But the sea has a funny way of stirring more than just the tides. It brings unexpected turns, surprising encounters, and sometimes, someone who makes you laugh again—really laugh.

That someone was Sean. What began as polite conversation in a corridor turned into shared breakfasts, theatre seats, long walks in Norwegian drizzle, and quiet evenings with cake and music. We weren't a whirlwind romance. We were a slow burn. A comforting warmth. Proof that companionship can find you at the moment you least expect it—and need it most.

This story is our story. A little messy, a little magical, and very much real. It's about two people who boarded a ship alone and disembarked not quite the same. To anyone out there who's thinking of doing something bold—taking that solo trip, striking up that conversation, or dancing in the aisle one last time—I hope this book reminds you that it's never too late for a new beginning.

Foreword

By Sean

I'll admit it—when I signed up for a solo cruise, I pictured a quiet fortnight of books, buffets, and the occasional polite chat with fellow travelers over lukewarm coffee. What I didn't expect was Samatha.

She wasn't flashy. She wasn't loud. She was real. The kind of person who notices the smallest details—a smudge on a wine glass, a funny typo in the daily newsletter, the exact shade of grey the sky turns before rain. And yet somehow, she missed the biggest detail of all: how lovely she was to be around.

From awkward introductions over buffet trays to dancing in the aisles during a Motown tribute show, we built something simple and honest. No pressure. No expectations. Just two people sharing stories, laughter, and more than a few slices of cake.

They say travel reveals character. What this cruise revealed to me was that connection doesn't need fireworks to be unforgettable. Sometimes, it's found in shared umbrellas, lost luggage, and a borrowed pen at breakfast.

To those reading this: take the trip. Say yes to the new tablemate. Watch the sunset—even in the rain. You never know who you might find standing beside you.

Table of Contents

Acknowledgement   7

Foreword   8

Chapter 1: Departure Tilbury, London   15

Sean and Samantha meet on deck as the ship glides away
from Tilbury. A shared appreciation for the crisp air, and a
small act of kindness. Samantha helping Sean with a
camera setting, sparks the first thread of connection.

Chapter 2: Open Waters   19

The North Sea stretches endlessly. The ship buzzes with
new friendships, music, and dancing. Sean and Samantha
dine at the same table, share stories of their younger days,
and discover a shared love of history.

Chapter 3: Haugesund   25

Exploring the quaint streets of Haugesund, they walk side
by side. Sean takes pictures of Samantha laughing in the
wind. They find warmth in a seaside café, sipping cocoa
and talking about love lost and found.

Chapter 4: Alesund   29

The art nouveau architecture charms them. They climb the
Aksla viewpoint together. At the summit, they watch the
sun set into the fjord, and Sean gently takes Samantha's
hand.

Chapter 5: Trondheim   33

They tour Nidaros Cathedral. Sean reveals he once
dreamed of being an architect. Samantha tells him about
her years teaching literature. That night, they dance
slowly at the Captain's Gala.

Chapter 6: Alta Begins 39

They cross the Arctic Circle. The excitement on the ship builds. In Alta, they chase the Northern Lights for the first time. Though clouds hide them, the night feels magical.

Chapter 7: Alta Awakens 49

On a husky sledding trip, Samantha's laughter fills the cold air. That night, the skies explode with green and violet ribbons. Sean and Samantha stand in awe, and share a kiss under the aurora.

Chapter 8: Tromsø's Touch 55

In Tromsø, they visit the Arctic Cathedral and Polaria. Sean opens up about his late wife. Samantha talks about her divorce and years spent alone. They realize they're healing together.

Chapter 9: At Sea 61

They spend a quiet day at sea. In a lounge filled with soft piano music, they talk about what comes next. The air between them is gentle, intimate.

Chapter 10: Narvik's Silence 69

Narvik's war museum stirs emotions. They walk through snow-dusted streets. Sean buys Samantha a delicate brooch shaped like a snowflake.

Chapter 11: Bodø's Beauty 79

Exploring the Saltstraumen and Bodø's rugged coast, they hike and take photos. Samantha shares her poetry. Sean is moved, and asks to hear more.

Chapter 12: Reflections
91

Another day at sea. They spend time in the spa, reading and holding hands. They talk about family, dreams deferred, and what love means after seventy.

Chapter 13: Bergen's Rain
107

They wander Bergen's old wharf in the rain. It's romantic, like a movie. In a small restaurant, they toast to second chances and dance one more time.

Chapter 14: Farewell Approaches
123

Back at sea, they sit in their favorite lounge. Friends they've made on the cruise wish them well. Sean gives Samantha a small photo album of their trip.

Chapter 15: Tilbury, London
137

Back where they started, they disembark. But their journey isn't over. They part with plans to meet again.

Epilogue
155

Sean and Samantha walk through Kew Gardens in London. The cherry blossoms are in full bloom. They're planning a trip to Vienna. The Northern Lights may have faded, but their love shines brightly.

CHAPTER 1

Departure

Tilbury, London – November 1, 2024

The ship loomed large and proud at the terminal, its decks already alive with passengers snapping photos, waving to loved ones, and marveling at the voyage ahead. The temperature hovered between 9 and 15°C, a misty gray veil wrapping the air in gentle coolness. Light winds ruffled coats and scarves, but the mood was festive. Dress code signage reminded guests to dress casually but avoid shorts and sleeveless tops in the restaurants.

Sean stood at the rail, his camera slung around his neck, capturing the pale sunlight breaking through the morning clouds. He hadn't taken a trip like this since Helen passed five years ago. It felt strange, liberating, and oddly lonely.

At 2 PM, after a smooth check-in, Sean collected his cruise card—a sleek plastic key to the days ahead—and stepped aboard with cautious optimism

Samantha, having just received her own card, looked around the bustling atrium with wide eyes. The chandeliers shimmered like droplets of starlight, and a soft murmur of music drifted from somewhere deeper in the ship.

Samantha arrived at the promenade deck just as the ship gave its deep, sonorous horn. She wore a burgundy scarf and carried a leather-bound notebook tucked under her arm. She'd spent the morning reading in the lounge but couldn't resist the pull of the open air as the ship began its journey.

They met near the stern, both drawn to the same stretch of railing. Samantha noticed Sean fiddling with the settings on his DSLR, frowning under his flat cap.

"ISO too high," she said gently, nodding toward the camera. "You'll get better light if you let the aperture work a little more."

Sean looked at her in surprise, then smiled. "You know cameras?"

"Taught photography club at the school for nearly twenty years," she said, holding out her hand. "Samantha."

"Sean. Pleased to meet you."

They shook hands, and the cold breeze sent a shiver down both their spines. Samantha chuckled and wrapped her scarf tighter.

"First time to Norway?" Sean asked.

"Yes, and chasing the Northern Lights is on my list. Always dreamed of it. You?"

"Same. My late wife and I talked about it for years. Took me a while to gather the courage."

Samantha gave a sympathetic nod. "Sometimes we have to carry their dreams, too."

They stood in companionable silence for a moment, the ship steadily moving downriver. Below them, gulls wheeled and cried. The shoreline slipped away slowly, replaced by the vast open promise of sea.

"Would you join me for dinner tonight?" Sean asked, surprising himself.

Samantha tilted her head. "I'd like that. But only if you bring your camera. I want to see what kind of trouble you get into with the settings."

Sean laughed, a warm sound carried away by the wind. "Deal."

Their journey had begun.

At 4:30 PM, as required under SOLAS (Safety Of Life at Sea) regulations, a mandatory guest safety drill took place. The ship's alarm bells rang out, followed by calm but firm announcements instructing all guests to proceed to their designated assembly stations. Sean and Samantha, along with hundreds of other passengers, made their way to the Palladium Show Lounge on Decks 7 and 8. Other guests gathered at the Purple Turtle Pub on Deck 8, and the Botanical Lounge and Raffles Bar on Deck

7. The staff guided them with precision, checking cruise cards and giving clear instructions on life jacket use, emergency protocols, and evacuation routes.

Though the atmosphere remained calm, the seriousness of the drill reminded everyone that safety was the foundation of the journey ahead. Sean appreciated the clarity and professionalism, while Samantha took mental notes, her teacher's instinct kicking in. They found themselves standing side by side once again, exchanging glances during the demonstration, comforted by each other's presence in the sea of unfamiliar faces.

That evening, the Buckingham Restaurant on Deck 7 was a warm oasis of candlelight and soft jazz. The maître d' welcomed them with a graceful nod and led them to a table near the panoramic windows. The sea, now a sheet of dark velvet, shimmered beneath a star-salted sky.

Samantha looked elegant in a navy blouse that caught the light when she moved. Sean had changed into a crisp shirt and blazer, his camera hanging proudly at his side.

They shared a bottle of Bordeaux and indulged in a three-course meal— lobster bisque for Samantha, a filet of sole for Sean, and shared crème brûlée that cracked under the tap of their spoons.

"This feels...unexpected," Samantha said, watching the flame of the candle dance between them. "But lovely."

"The best kind of surprise," Sean agreed. "I thought I'd be dining alone, editing photos in my cabin."

"And I thought I'd be scribbling in my notebook, nursing a glass of wine. Funny how quickly things change."

After dinner, they wandered toward the Botanical Lounge, drawn by the soft strains of live piano music. The lounge was a glass-domed haven filled with hanging greenery and soft amber lighting. It smelled faintly of orchids and citrus.

They found seats beneath a flowering trellis. Sean ordered them elderflower cocktails—light, fragrant, and gently fizzy.

Samantha leaned back, watching the pianist glide effortlessly over the keys. "I used to play a little, in college. Then life took over."

"Do you miss it?"

"Sometimes. But tonight, I think I'd rather just listen."

Sean raised his glass. "To new beginnings, then."

Samantha clinked hers gently against his. "To what's still ahead."

The music swelled softly around them as they sat in quiet joy. Outside the lounge's glass dome, stars wheeled over the North Sea. Inside, two hearts, once adrift, found their way back to the warmth of possibility.

Sean stepped into his stateroom and placed his camera gently on the desk. The hum of the ship was soothing, a low heartbeat in the silence. He looked at the empty armchair across from his bed and, for the first time in years, didn't feel the sting of solitude. There was a warmth lingering from the evening—a smile still hovering on his lips, a faint scent of elderflower on his breath. He sat on the edge of the bed, gazing at the photos he'd taken that day. But it wasn't the pictures of the ship or the sea he kept returning to—it was the one he'd taken, almost unconsciously, of Samantha's hands resting gently on her notebook.

In her cabin down the corridor, Samantha hung her scarf on a hook and took a deep breath. Her cheeks still carried the faint flush of laughter. She poured herself a small glass of water and sat at the writing desk, opening her notebook. But for once, she didn't write. Instead, she stared out the porthole, watching the sea stretch into darkness. A quiet thrill buzzed in her chest—one she hadn't felt in decades. The way Sean looked at her, listened to her, respected her pace—it was all so new, yet familiar, like stepping into a half-forgotten dream.

She smiled to herself, closing the notebook. Maybe tomorrow, she would write about the sky, the sea... and the man with the camera who noticed her.

CHAPTER 2

A New Horizon

At Sea – November 2, 2024

The second morning at sea brought with it a welcome change in weather. The temperature settled between 8 and 11°C, with sunny intervals peeking through the scattered clouds. A fresh breeze danced across the open decks, carrying with it the salty scent of the North Sea. Sunrise arrived promptly at 6:25 AM, casting a golden glow across the water, while sunset was predicted for 4:30 PM, leaving a long, cozy evening ahead.

Samantha rose early, as always, her inner clock never quite adjusting to retirement. She wrapped herself in a soft shawl and stepped out onto the promenade deck, breathing in the crisp morning air. The sea sparkled with the promise of the day, and she clutched her coffee close as she watched the horizon shift.

Sean, too, was up before most. He'd already taken a stroll along the upper deck and captured a few shots of the sunrise—the golden light kissing the tips of waves, a solitary gull slicing through the sky. He wasn't usually one for early mornings, but something about the sea awakened an old hunger in him—the desire to see, to feel, to live.

From 7:30 to 10 AM, they both visited the Borough Market buffet on Deck 12 for breakfast, enjoying a wide variety of morning offerings. Samantha chose a bowl of muesli with fresh fruit and a warm croissant, while Sean indulged in a full English breakfast—bacon, eggs, grilled tomatoes, and a hearty cup of tea. They didn't dine together that morning, but their paths crossed briefly near the coffee machine. A shared smile, a warm "Good morning," and then they returned to their tables, slowly weaving their routines around each other.

By mid-morning, the ship buzzed with quiet activity. Guests lounged with books in cozy corners, explored the boutique shops, or participated in lectures about the ports ahead. Samantha attended a short session on Norwegian folklore, taking notes with her ever-present pencil. Sean wandered the ship with his camera, capturing small moments—a couple playing chess, a steward arranging flowers, the glint of sun through etched glass.

That afternoon, Sean decided to purchase a drinks package, giving him access to a wide selection of wines, beers, and spirits for £22.95 per person per night. He figured he might as well enjoy himself fully, and he looked forward to trying new cocktails over dinner. Samantha, preferring a simpler indulgence, opted for the water package. For £17.95, she had unlimited access to still or sparkling water—just what she needed to accompany her meals and daily reading sessions.

That afternoon, Sean decided to purchase a drinks package, giving him access to a wide selection of wines, beers, and spirits for £22.95 per person per night. He figured he might as well enjoy himself fully, and he looked forward to trying new cocktails over dinner. Samantha, preferring a simpler indulgence, opted for the water package. For £17.95, she had unlimited access to still or sparkling water—just what she needed to accompany her meals and daily reading sessions.

Lunch was served from 12 to 2 PM, also at Borough Market on Deck 12. Samantha enjoyed a light salad with smoked salmon and dill dressing, followed by a lemon tart. Sean, always with a bigger appetite, went for lamb stew with root vegetables and crusty bread. They sat a few tables apart, close enough to exchange a few words about the food and the gentle sway of the ship. Their comfort with each other was growing—a quiet companionship born from shared presence rather than forced conversation.

After lunch, they both made their way to the Observatory Lounge for a Line Dance class. The floor quickly filled with laughing guests of all ages, attempting to follow the instructor's energetic movements. Samantha surprised Sean with her rhythm and coordination, and he found himself enjoying the music and camaraderie more than he expected. They danced, stumbled, laughed, and danced some more—moving not perfectly, but joyfully.

At 2:15 PM, they took seats in the Palladium for the guest lecture: "Northern Sea & Northern Lights." The speaker, a seasoned Arctic expedition leader, captivated the audience with stories of celestial light shows, polar wildlife, and ancient Norse legends tied to the aurora borealis. Samantha took diligent notes, while Sean leaned back, absorbing the images and sounds with a peaceful smile. Occasionally, their eyes met with shared wonder, each knowing they were creating memories that would stay with them long after the cruise ended.

Anticipation hummed in the air for the evening ahead. Tonight, the dress code was formal. Men were expected in dinner jackets or lounge suits, and ladies in elegant trousers or cocktail dresses. It was the ship's first Gala Night, and the Buckingham Restaurant was set to serve its most exquisite menu yet.

To mark the occasion, the Captain's Welcome Reception was scheduled—a traditional and cherished event aboard cruise ships. Guests would be introduced to the ship's Master and senior officers in a formal ceremony held in the grand Palladium. For first seating guests, the doors opened at 5 PM; for second seating guests, at 7 PM. Attendees had the chance to take a commemorative photograph with the Captain before receiving a complimentary drink. As glasses were raised, the Captain introduced his officers on stage, each greeted with applause. The room sparkled with smiles, sequins, and a sense of shared adventure.

Tonight was the Captain's Welcome Reception, a time-honored tradition on cruise ships. The Palladium's doors opened at 5 PM for first-seating guests, and Sean and Samantha were among the first to arrive. A queue formed for photographs with Captain Henrik Sørensen, who greeted each guest warmly.

After their photograph, they were handed complimentary glasses of champagne and took their seats in the grand theatre. The captain appeared on stage shortly after, introducing his senior officers amid warm applause. The atmosphere was celebratory and elegant, filled with the soft clink of glasses and the hum of conversation.

Samantha spent time choosing her outfit—a deep emerald dress that matched her eyes, with a silver shawl she hadn't worn in years. As she applied a touch of lipstick, she looked at herself in the mirror and smiled softly. It felt good to dress up. It felt good to be seen.

Sean opted for a charcoal-gray suit, neatly pressed, paired with a crisp white shirt and navy tie. He considered the cufflinks Helen had given him once—tiny compasses—but chose instead the simpler ones he'd worn to his daughter's wedding. Tonight felt important, but not nostalgic. It felt like the beginning of something new.

They met near the central staircase, both pausing as they caught sight of each other. Samantha's eyes widened just a little, and Sean's lips tugged into a smile.

"You look stunning," he said.

"You clean up quite well yourself," she replied, slipping her arm through his. "Shall we?"

Dinner was a grand affair. The Buckingham Restaurant glowed with chandeliers and the shimmer of crystal glasses. Waiters in white gloves moved like dancers, and a string quartet played softly near the entrance. Sean and Samantha shared another delightful meal—beef Wellington for him, roasted sea bass for her—paired with a velvety Pinot Noir.

Conversation flowed easily between them. They spoke of books and travels, of their grown children and youthful regrets. They laughed—often—and paused in moments of thoughtful silence. Around them, other couples toasted, celebrated anniversaries, or simply soaked in the elegance.

After dessert, they made their way to the Observatory Lounge for a nightcap. The panoramic windows offered a sweeping view of the sea beneath the starlit sky. The wind had quieted some, and the waves rolled gently beneath them.

Samantha sipped her amaretto, a flush of warmth in her cheeks. "Do you ever wonder," she asked, "how much life we still have left to live?"

Sean looked at her, thoughtful. "Not as often as I should. But this trip... it makes me think I've only just started again."

She reached across the small table and touched his hand briefly. "Then let's live it well."

The music, the sea, the promise of the journey—they all mingled in the air like a quiet blessing.

And in that moment, neither of them felt old. They only felt alive.

Later that evening, they made their way back to the Palladium for the live show—*Masquerade*. The grand theatre was filled with guests dressed to impress, the ambiance echoing the timeless elegance of Vienna itself. The performance was a dazzling blend of modern musical theatre and classical artistry, set against the romantic backdrop of a masked ball. Vocalists in elaborate costumes delivered exclusive arrangements with haunting beauty and powerful harmony, as dancers glided across the stage in a swirl of velvet and mystery.

Samantha was transfixed, her eyes shining as she watched the masked performers weave their tale of love and longing. Sean, beside her, was equally captivated—not just by the performance, but by the woman next to him. He stole glances at her, the soft theatre lights highlighting the joy in her expression.

As the final note lingered in the air and the curtain fell to thunderous applause, they turned to each other, smiling.

"That was incredible," Samantha whispered.

"Unforgettable," Sean agreed.

They lingered in their seats for a moment longer, savoring the magic of the show—and perhaps, the magic beginning to blossom between them.

But the evening was not yet over.

At the Observatory Lounge, the mood shifted to something more playful and electric. The theatre show company singers took the stage once more, this time with glimmering jumpsuits and high energy. It was the ABBA Cabaret, and they were calling all "Super Troupers" and "Dancing Queens" to join them.

The first notes of "Mamma Mia" rang out, and Samantha squealed with delight. "I love this song!" she said, pulling Sean by the hand.

Though slightly hesitant at first, Sean followed her onto the dance floor. Surrounded by fellow guests clapping and twirling, they moved to the infectious beat. Samantha danced with joyful abandon, and Sean—laughing, clapping, and eventually spinning her under his arm—felt years melt away.

They danced through "Waterloo," "Take a Chance on Me," and "Dancing Queen," their feet growing tired but their spirits soaring. The crowd was alive, voices singing along, arms in the air, laughter echoing through the night.

By the time the show ended, and the last refrain faded into a chorus of cheers, it was half past midnight. They were breathless, exhilarated, and utterly content.

As they made their way back to their cabins, their hands brushed briefly before letting go.

"Goodnight, Sean," Samantha said softly at her door.

"Goodnight, Samantha," he replied. "Sweet dreams."

And for the first time in a long time, they both knew their dreams would be filled not with memories of the past—but the hope of what was still to come.

CHAPTER 3

Drizzle and Discovery

Haugesund, Norway – November 3, 2024

The morning light arrived late in Haugesund, Norway, with the sun rising at 8:04 AM. By then, the Ship had already docked at Garpaskjær Quay, a modest yet welcoming berth nestled at the edge of this coastal town. A fine drizzle misted the air, mingling with a fresh breeze that swept across the ship's decks. Temperatures hovered between 9 and 13°C—cool, damp, and perfect for layers.

Sean and Samantha awoke to the soft patter of rain against their cabin windows. The previous night's glamour gave way to the ship's designated casual dress code, and both welcomed the comfort of warm sweaters and sensible shoes. After dressing, they made their way once again to Borough Market on Deck 12 for breakfast.

The familiar hum of morning activity greeted them. Samantha filled her plate with warm oatmeal, sliced bananas, and a drizzle of honey. Sean, drawn as always to the heartier options, selected a mushroom omelette and rye toast. They shared a table by the window this time, watching as the drizzle blurred the outlines of Haugesund's hills beyond the quay.

"Looks like we might need our raincoats today," Samantha said with a smile, sipping her coffee.

Sean nodded, glancing at the grey sky. "And umbrellas, if we're brave enough to wander."

They laughed softly, finishing their breakfast before heading back to their cabins to prepare for their first onshore excursion. As they dressed, they each tucked their cruise cards safely into jacket pockets—a small but critical step. The cards were not only their onboard ID and payment method, but also essential for going ashore. No cruise card, no passage through the gangway.

A complimentary shuttle bus service provided by the port authority operated that day, running every 30 minutes. The fare was NOK 80 per person, and the drop-off and pick-up point was at Vår Frelsers Church, a central landmark in town. The first shuttle departed the ship at 9:30 AM, with the last return from town scheduled for 3:00 PM.

By 10 AM, the drizzle had lightened slightly, and a line of passengers, clad in waterproofs and holding umbrellas like miniature sails, waited patiently to board the shuttle. Samantha and Sean joined them, sitting close as the small bus hummed toward the town center.

Haugesund greeted them with quiet charm. The town's streets glistened under the rain, and pastel houses reflected softly in the wet cobblestones. Shops with glowing windows offered refuge, their interiors filled with wool sweaters, handcrafted souvenirs, and the scent of cinnamon pastries.

They wandered through the harbor district, umbrellas bumping gently as they walked side-by-side. Sean paused often to photograph fishing boats bobbing in the water, their colors vivid against the grey. Samantha, always curious, ducked into a small bookstore, where the owner greeted her in gentle Norwegian and offered her a paperback in English about Viking queens.

They regrouped near the local church, its stone spire cutting through the mist. Bells rang out the hour, and they stood for a moment, listening.

"I could stay here a while," Sean said, quietly.

"Me too," Samantha replied. "It has that sort of peace, doesn't it?"

They stopped for lunch at a quaint café, sharing a bowl of creamy fish soup and fresh bread. A candle flickered between them, and outside the drizzle began to slow.

By mid-afternoon, they boarded the shuttle for the return journey, just in time for the final 3 PM departure. Once back aboard the ship, they scanned their cruise cards and were greeted by the familiar warmth of the. The contrast to the chilled dampness outside was immediate and comforting.

By mid-afternoon, they boarded the shuttle for the return journey, just in time for the final 3 PM departure. Once back aboard the ship, they scanned their cruise cards and were greeted by the familiar warmth of the Ship. The contrast to the chilled dampness outside was immediate and comforting.

Feeling pleasantly tired but still enjoying each other's company, they decided to grab a casual bite at the Alfresco Pizza Grill on Deck 12. The smell of freshly baked pizza welcomed them, and they took a seat under the sheltered awning, looking out over the rain-slick deck. Samantha chose a Margherita slice, while Sean went for pepperoni, both paired with a light soda. It was simple, satisfying, and felt like the perfect way to ease back into shipboard life.

Afterwards, they strolled over to Borough Market once more, this time to enjoy afternoon cream tea. A warm pot of English breakfast tea, scones with clotted cream and jam, and a few delicate finger sandwiches offered a gentle indulgence. They sat quietly, watching as other passengers drifted in, sharing nods and soft smiles.

Later in the afternoon, they made their way to the Aces & Eights room, where card and board games were set up for guests. The cozy, carpeted space echoed with gentle laughter and quiet strategy. Sean introduced Samantha to a game of cribbage, which she picked up quickly. They shared playful jabs and delighted in the simplicity of an old-fashioned pastime, surrounded by fellow cruisers similarly engaged.

At 4:15 PM, they walked to the Palladium for a destination experiences presentation focused on Alta, their upcoming port of call. The theatre slowly filled as guests settled into the plush seats. A destination expert took the stage, accompanied by visuals and maps. The talk covered Alta's unique location within the Arctic Circle, the chances of viewing the Northern Lights, and cultural highlights including the Sami heritage and UNESCO-listed rock carvings.

Sean and Samantha listened intently, exchanging occasional glances, already imagining the crisp polar air and glowing skies ahead.

Dinner that evening was a step up in elegance. They dined at the Buckingham Restaurant, a refined venue on Deck 7. The décor was warm and classic, with crisp white linens, soft lighting, and a menu featuring slow-cooked lamb shank, grilled salmon, and seasonal vegetables. Sean ordered the lamb, while Samantha opted for the salmon, both pairing their meals with a modest glass of red wine.

They lingered over dessert—Sean with his sticky toffee pudding and Samantha savoring a lemon tart—enjoying the easy rhythm of conversation that came so naturally now.

After dinner, they made their way to the Palladium Theatre for the evening's main entertainment: a comedy performance by David Huband. Known for his firebrand style of humor and musical parodies, Huband took the stage with a guitar slung over his shoulder and a grin that promised mischief. His routine included cheeky songs and sharp-witted satire, poking fun at everything from cruise ship etiquette to romantic misadventures. The audience roared with laughter, and Sean and Samantha found themselves chuckling until tears gathered in the corners of their eyes.

Not quite ready to return to their cabins, they decided to cap the night with some live music at Raffles Bar. The intimate lounge on Deck 7 was dimly lit, its ambiance warm and sophisticated. At the grand piano sat Callum Bradley, the ship's resident pianist, his fingers gliding effortlessly across the keys. He played familiar standards—jazz classics, gentle ballads, and a few spirited show tunes that had guests swaying softly in their seats. Sean ordered a nightcap, while Samantha sipped sparkling water with a twist of lime. They sat in companionable silence, absorbing the music and the low murmur of contentment around them.

As the ship prepared to sail again, Samantha stood on deck with Sean beside her. Lights flickered in the town below, and the drizzle returned, more a mist than a rain. They stood in silence, wrapped in scarves and the growing comfort of companionship.

Another port, another memory.

And in the quiet hum of the departing ship, they could both sense it:

Something beautiful was beginning.

CHAPTER 4

Fjords and Formalities

Ålesund, Norway – November 4, 2024

The Ship glided gracefully into the harbor at Ålesund, docking at Sørsida Quay just as the town began to stir. The sky was painted with soft hues of silver and pink as the sun rose at 8:19 AM, casting reflections onto the glassy waters that surrounded this art nouveau gem of the Norwegian coast.

The weather remained true to form for early November—temperatures ranged from 8 to 12°C, with a drizzle gently falling and a light breeze sweeping through the air. Samantha and Sean woke early, drawn by the promise of a new town to explore. After dressing in warm layers and waterproof jackets, they met once again at Borough Market on Deck 12 for breakfast, as had quickly become their morning ritual.

The buffet was familiar and comforting. Samantha selected a croissant, scrambled eggs, and a slice of smoked salmon, while Sean filled his plate with crispy bacon, sautéed mushrooms, and a Danish pastry. They sat together at their usual table near the windows, which provided a panoramic view of the town's charming buildings nestled between fjords and hills.

"It's like a storybook painting," Samantha said, sipping her tea as the drizzle misted the glass.

"It is," Sean replied. "Even the weather fits the mood. Cozy and a little mysterious."

After breakfast, they prepared for their day ashore. Their cruise cards safely tucked into coat pockets, they disembarked the ship by late morning. The pier buzzed with fellow passengers, all dressed in weatherproof layers and filled with anticipation. Sørsida Quay, the berth for the day, was a short walk from the heart of Ålesund, which allowed guests to explore independently without shuttle service.

Sean and Samantha wandered down cobbled streets lined with pastel-colored buildings and whimsical towers. Ålesund's famed Art Nouveau architecture gave the city an old-world charm, while cozy cafés and boutique shops beckoned from each corner. They paused at a harbor café, ducking inside to share a hot chocolate topped with whipped cream and to warm their hands.

Afterward, they walked to the base of Mount Aksla, where the famous 418-step staircase leads to a viewpoint overlooking the town. They didn't climb the full staircase—mindful of slippery steps—but they explored the park at the base, taking photos and chatting with other travelers.

By late afternoon, they continued their afternoon with cream tea at Borough Market, indulging in scones with clotted cream and jam, and a shared pot of Earl Grey. In addition to the cream tea, there were other traditional offerings for afternoon tea, including a selection of biscuits, small cakes, and freshly brewed coffee. The comforting warmth of the drinks and sweet treats made it a cozy moment of rest after their outdoor adventure.

Still energized, they made their way to the ship's game show event, *Time Drop*, held in the main lounge. The game was fast-paced and filled with laughter as contestants raced against a ticking clock to answer questions and stop the drop. Sean and Samantha cheered enthusiastically from the audience, caught up in the excitement and suspense.

Before heading to dinner, they stopped at the Botanical Lounge for a session of live classical music titled *Classical Inspirations*. The atmosphere was serene, with a string quartet playing gentle arrangements of timeless pieces. Samantha and Sean sat quietly with glasses of sparkling water and wine, letting the calming melodies wash over them.

With the formal dress code reinstated for the evening—dinner jackets or lounge suits for men, cocktail dresses or trousers for ladies—they returned to their cabins to change. Sean wore a charcoal grey suit with a navy tie, while Samantha selected a deep plum dress with subtle embroidery.

Dinner followed at Saffron, the ship's specialty Indian restaurant, where they experienced the culinary delights of Kerala. The executive chef had crafted a three-course menu that highlighted the vibrant flavors of southern India. For starters, they shared crispy vegetable samosas and prawns with coconut chutney. Samantha chose the Kerala fish curry as her main, while Sean delighted in a fragrant lamb rogan josh. The meal ended with sweet cardamom-spiced gulab jamun and mango kulfi. The aromatic spices and warm ambiance made it an unforgettable dining experience.

Following dinner, they returned to the Palladium for the evening's live theatre show: *Committed to the Brothers' Blue*. The performance was a high-energy romp filled with music, humor, and drama. It told the story of the Brothers Blue on a fast-paced mission to raise money for orphanages while being chased by the law and a very dodgy mayor. With toe-tapping tunes, comedic chase scenes, and heartfelt moments, the audience was swept into the whirlwind adventure. Sean and Samantha laughed out loud throughout the show, thoroughly entertained.

After the theatre show, they stepped out into the softly lit corridor, savoring the buzz from the performance. "So," Samantha said, turning to Sean with a twinkle in her eye, "do we continue the night with Party Tunes Floor Fillers at the Observatory, or do we take it easy with Callum Bradley's live piano at Raffles Bar?"

Sean chuckled, pretending to weigh the options with dramatic flair. "Hmm, dancing or mellow melodies? What's your vote?"

"I could use a little groove, but I also wouldn't mind unwinding with a cocktail and some smooth tunes," she replied.

"How about we stop by both? Catch a few songs at Raffles, and if the mood strikes, head up to the Observatory later?"

"Perfect," she smiled.

They strolled off, ready to see where the night would take them.

As they returned to their cabins later, walking together down the quiet corridor, they lingered for a moment outside Samantha's door.

"Today was… perfect," she said softly.

Sean nodded. "It really was. I'm glad we're sharing this."

"Me too," she whispered.

They said goodnight, and though they retired to separate cabins, neither of them slept quickly.

Because something gentle and extraordinary was unfolding between them.

CHAPTER 5

A Taste of Elegance

At Sea, Norway – November 5, 2024

The Ship sailed steadily north through the Norwegian Sea as Sean and Samantha allowed themselves a slower pace after the excitement of Ålesund. With temperatures between 6 and 11°C, the day brought light rain and a fresh breeze. The sun rose at 8:25 AM and would disappear again by 4:21 PM. The air held the promise of a chillier evening, and the passengers adapted their wardrobe accordingly. The dress code for the day was elegant: smart suits or jackets with or without ties for men, and cocktail dresses or trouser suits for ladies.

Sean and Samantha awoke later than usual, the gentle rocking of the ship and the previous night's events lulling them into a deeper rest. They decided to forgo breakfast, opting instead for a more luxurious lunch at the Buckingham Restaurant. At 12:30 PM, they met outside the entrance on Deck 7, both dressed smartly for the day's formal tone.

Sean looked dashing in a navy blue tailored suit with a crisp white shirt and a burgundy silk tie that added a pop of color. His leather shoes were polished to a fine shine, and a silver watch peeked out from beneath his cuff. Samantha was equally elegant in a midnight blue cocktail dress that shimmered subtly under the light. The dress featured a modest V-neckline and a flowing skirt that reached just below her knees. She paired it with a pearl necklace, small earrings, and silver kitten heels, completing a look of understated sophistication.

In the morning, the ship was already abuzz with activity. Guests gathered at Centre Court for a lively fruits and vegetables carving demonstration. Samantha was fascinated by the intricacy and artistry displayed, while Sean admired the chef's quick hands and clever techniques. It was a relaxing and inspiring start to the day.

Following the demonstration, they made their way to the Palladium Theatre for the morning guest lecture. Dr. Ed Derbyshire, an expert in space science, delivered a compelling talk titled "When Things Go Wrong in Space." He recounted tales of near-disasters and the resilience of astronauts in the face of mechanical failure and cosmic unpredictability. Sean, a lifelong enthusiast of science and history, was thoroughly captivated, and Samantha appreciated the dramatic human element behind the scientific storytelling.

Later in the day, Sean attended another guest lecture at the Palladium titled "Surprising Discoveries" with Peter Young. The talk explored little-known historical findings and quirky scientific moments that changed the way we understand the world. Sean found it intellectually stimulating, his mind buzzing with curiosity and delight.

Meanwhile, Samantha opted for something more introspective and personal. She attended the Friends of Bill W Meet in the Partnerships Area, a supportive gathering offering quiet camaraderie and heartfelt sharing. The session gave her a peaceful space to reflect and connect, grounding her in a sense of community even while at sea.

When they met up afterward, their conversation flowed easily.

"Peter Young really knows how to make history feel alive," Sean said. "There's always something new to learn, isn't there?"

Samantha smiled. "I didn't go to the lecture. I went to the Friends of Bill W meet. It was exactly what I needed—some meaningful connection and quiet time."

Sean nodded with understanding. "That's important. Sometimes it's not about learning something new but remembering what grounds us."

Inside the Buckingham Restaurant, the ambiance was refined—white linen tablecloths, sparkling glassware, and soft instrumental music in the background. Sean ordered a tomato bisque to start, followed by roasted duck with honey glaze and root vegetables. Samantha chose a smoked salmon starter and a vegetarian risotto with wild mushrooms for her main. Their dessert of choice was a delicate crème brûlée, its sugary crust cracking under the lightest touch of a spoon.

"This makes up for missing breakfast," Sean said with a satisfied sigh, sipping a glass of sparkling water.

"I think we did it right," Samantha agreed, smiling over her cup of herbal tea.

After lunch, they enjoyed a gentle stroll along the indoor promenade before returning to the Buckingham Restaurant at 3:30 PM for the Wine Tasting Experience. Hosted by the ship's sommelier, the tasting took them through a curated journey of global wines—from crisp Chardonnays to rich Malbecs. Guests were taught to swirl, sniff, and sip while noting the unique characteristics of each vintage. Sean favored a bold Italian red, while Samantha leaned toward a lightly oaked white from the Loire Valley.

Their cheeks warmed from the wine and their conversation filled with laughter, Sean and Samantha lingered at the end of the event, chatting with fellow guests and exchanging impressions of the various pairings.

As the day transitioned into evening, they returned to their cabins to prepare for the formal night ahead, the promise of elegance and romance shimmering just ahead on the horizon.

While Sean returned to his cabin to rest and reflect, Samantha decided to indulge herself further. She made her way to the wellness area at Deck 2 Midship, where the sauna and steam room were open daily from 8 AM to 8 PM. After a few minutes of relaxing in the calming steam, she was welcomed into the spa for a rejuvenating treatment package.

Her chosen spa journey included an anti-aging facial, a soothing eye treatment, an Eastern head massage, a hot stone massage, and a refreshing foot and ankle massage. For just £66, it was a luxurious and invigorating experience that left her feeling both radiant and deeply relaxed. She emerged from the spa with glowing skin and a tranquil spirit, ready to dress for the formal evening ahead.

As the day transitioned into evening, they returned to their cabins to prepare for the formal night ahead, the promise of elegance and romance shimmering just ahead on the horizon.

At dinner, they found themselves weighing options. The Surf 'N' Turf— an indulgent combination of handcrafted filet mignon and lobster tail— was available for a supplement of £21. It sounded tempting.

"Lobster and steak," Sean mused. "That's not something I have every day."

Samantha tilted her head thoughtfully. "It does sound lovely, but the three-course meal here is already so satisfying—and it's included."

In the end, they opted for the three-course meal at the Buckingham Restaurant, enjoying fresh seasonal dishes without the extra charge. They agreed the food was impeccable, and the experience, with its fine service and comfortable elegance, was just as memorable.

After dinner, they made their way to the theatre for the evening's performance at the Palladium. The featured production was *Abigail's Party*, a sharply observed suburban comedy set in 1970s Britain. The story unfolded with biting satire, chronicling the aspirations and tastes of the new middle class. As they watched the tension, awkwardness, and hilarity unfold on stage, Sean and Samantha exchanged knowing smiles, appreciating both the humor and the subtle critique woven through the show.

The performance concluded to enthusiastic applause, and the couple lingered for a moment in the aisle, chatting with fellow guests who also relished the nostalgic yet relevant themes.

"Some things never change," Sean remarked with a chuckle.

Samantha grinned. "And thankfully, some things—like a good laugh— always bring people together.

Not yet ready to call it a night, they continued their evening at Gianluca's Frank & Dean Tribute. Gianluca, dressed to the nines, delivered silky renditions of Frank Sinatra and Dean Martin classics. As the smooth crooning of "Fly Me to the Moon" and "That's Amore" filled the room, Sean and Samantha found themselves swaying slightly in their seats, lost in the timeless charm of the Rat Pack era.

After the tribute show, they headed to Tia's Party Cabaret, a late-night celebration pulsing with energy and delight. Colorful lights, vibrant costumes, and eclectic performances drew them in. Encouraged by the joyful atmosphere and catchy music, they danced with the crowd, moving with carefree abandon. They didn't leave the Observatory until half past midnight, hearts still light and feet slightly sore.

As they strolled back to their cabins under the soft hallway lights, Sean looked at Samantha and said with a laugh, "We're not too old for this after all."

Samantha chuckled, linking her arm with his. "Speak for yourself—I'm just getting started."

Two Solo Together

CHAPTER 6

History and Heartbeats

Trondheim, Norway – November 6, 2024

By the time the Ship slowly docked at the Sørsidekaiene berth in Trondheim at 8:00 AM, a gentle drizzle was already blanketing the historic city. The light wind carried the scent of damp stone and seawater, while the thermometer hovered between a chilly 2 and 6°C. Despite the gloomy sky, the day held the promise of discovery. All guests were required to be back on board by 5:30 PM for a 6:00 PM departure, and most, including Sean and Samantha, eagerly planned to make the most of their time ashore.

After a hearty breakfast at the Borough Market on Deck 12 — a ritual now firmly established — they made sure to bring their cruise cards, which were required to exit and re-enter the ship via the gangway. The cruise staff scanned them out, and they stepped onto the misty quay with excitement.

"This drizzle reminds me of London," Sean said, raising his collar.

"Only colder and with better views," Samantha replied with a wink.

Their first order of business was boarding the shuttle bus service provided by the port authority. The fare was free, and the journey into town was a smooth ride through the quaint streets of Trondheim, past pastel-painted buildings and views of the Nidelva River. The drop-off point was near citycentre at Leutherhaven, the iconic Nidaros Cathedral, just a short walk from Vår Frue Church, the designated shuttle hub.

They wandered through the town's cobbled streets, admiring the vibrant wooden warehouses along the wharves and stopping at small shops filled with wool garments, artisanal chocolates, and hand-carved wooden figurines. Samantha couldn't resist buying a pair of local woolen mittens, while Sean browsed vintage books in a quiet corner of an independent bookstore.

They visited several landmarks, beginning with Nidaros Cathedral, its Gothic spires rising through the mist with quiet grandeur. Inside, stained-glass windows filtered soft light onto ancient stone floors. Both were moved by the spiritual weight and artistry of the space. Not far from the cathedral, they stepped into Vår Frue Church, a smaller but equally atmospheric church with a serene interior and flickering votive candles.

Next, they explored the Archbishop's Palace Museum, located adjacent to the cathedral. There, they examined medieval artifacts, including ancient coins, religious relics, and detailed tapestries. The museum's layout told a captivating story of Trondheim's ecclesiastical and royal history, giving Sean and Samantha a deeper appreciation for the city's enduring heritage.

From there, they strolled through the Trondheim Museum of Art, where they enjoyed a range of contemporary and classical Norwegian works. Samantha was particularly drawn to a collection of impressionist landscapes that echoed the misty scenery outside, while Sean admired the intricacies of historical portraiture.

Before catching their shuttle, they wandered through the bustling fruit and vegetable market at Torvet, Trondheim's main square. Despite the drizzle, vendors displayed bright red berries, jars of jam, handmade sausages, and plump root vegetables. The scent of roasted nuts and spiced cider filled the air. Sean bought a bag of candied almonds while Samantha sampled a slice of cinnamon-scented apple cake.

Lunch was a simple affair—Norwegian open-faced sandwiches and hot coffee from a cozy café nestled in an alley. They shared a table with two Norwegian retirees who, despite the language barrier, chatted warmly and gestured at maps and photos.

"This city feels... timeless," Samantha whispered as they walked back toward the shuttle stop.

"It does," Sean agreed. "Quiet, but full of stories."

They caught the 3:00 PM shuttle back to the ship—the last one departing town—and stepped aboard just as the wind picked up again. Their cheeks were flushed with cold and satisfaction from the day's exploration.

Later that afternoon, they returned to the Borough Market for warm scones and spiced tea, the comfort of the familiar wrapping around them like a blanket. It was a quiet moment of reflection, with soft conversation and laughter between bites of cake.

As the ship pulled away from Trondheim's harbor that evening, Sean and Samantha stood side by side on Deck 12, wrapped in scarves and silence, watching the city's twinkling lights fade into the mist.

"Trondheim surprised me," Samantha said.

"In the best way," Sean nodded. "I'd come back."

They lingered there for a while, letting the cool air settle around them, hearts still warmed by the city's charm.

Back inside, the mood shifted as they wandered into a new conversation. With the ship now at sea again, the onboard casino on Deck 5 was open.

"I've never really tried my luck with slots," Sean admitted as they walked past the glittering lights and the electronic jingle of machines.

Samantha raised an eyebrow. "Not even once?"

"Well, maybe once. Years ago. Lost a fiver," he chuckled.

"I say we go for it," she said with a grin. "We've earned a little thrill after all that culture."

Sean looked uncertain. "It's not exactly my style."

"Oh, come on. We'll set a limit—£20 each. Strictly for fun."

He hesitated, and she nudged his arm playfully. "Unless you're scared I'll win more than you."

That did it. "Alright, alright. But don't blame me when we end up buying the next round of drinks with Monopoly money."

Their laughter echoed as they made their way toward the gaming floor, unsure of their luck, but certain that whatever the outcome, they'd enjoy the gamble—together.

The dress code for the day was casual, and both travelers dressed thoughtfully for the weather. Sean chose a grey wool coat layered over a navy-blue fleece and long-sleeved thermal shirt, paired with dark denim trousers and waterproof walking shoes. He added a knitted scarf and leather gloves for warmth, topping it off with a tweed flat cap that gave him an air of old-fashioned charm.

Samantha wore a plum-colored quilted coat with a faux-fur trimmed hood over a cozy cream sweater and corduroy trousers. A knitted hat pulled snug over her ears, and leather ankle boots with wool socks kept her feet warm. A paisley-patterned scarf added a touch of flair to her otherwise practical attire. She carried a crossbody bag with her essentials, including gloves, tissues, and her camera.

Later in the evening, as the ship gently rocked under the darkening Norwegian sky, Sean and Samantha found themselves browsing the dinner options posted on the digital display screens near the atrium.

"I've been thinking about that lobster again," Samantha said with a playful sigh. "And those grilled sea bass fillets."

Sean raised an eyebrow. "You really are set on that seafood dinner, aren't you?"

She grinned. "They promised fresh ingredients—Norwegian crab soup, king prawns, line-caught fish. It's practically an experience."

One menu in particular caught Samantha's eye: **Sea & Grass**, the ship's specialty restaurant nestled on Deck 12.

"Ooh, this sounds promising," she said, pointing. "Handcrafted filet mignon and lobster tail. A proper Surf 'n' Turf. And look, the chef's promising freshly sourced seafood."

He paused at the restaurant's entrance, where warm lighting and the aroma of herbs and butter wafted out. "£29.95 each though. That's more than a bit of a splurge."

Samantha looked at him seriously for a moment. "We've seen so much today. Walked through history, museums, markets... Isn't it nice to Sean squinted at the elegant menu. "£29.95 per person," he read aloud. "That's not a small commitment."

"Well, it's a one-time splurge," she replied. "We've been good, haven't we? All the included meals so far. Maybe this is the night to treat ourselves."

He hesitated, shifting his weight. "We've had lovely meals in Buckingham without extra cost. Three courses and excellent service. Is the lobster really going to taste *that* much fresher?"

Samantha gave him a sideways look. "You mean to say you don't miss a perfectly grilled steak and buttery lobster tail now and then?"

"Oh, I miss it," he admitted. "I just wonder if we're paying for the food—or the candlelight and linen napkins."

"Maybe both. And isn't that half the fun?" she countered.

Sean chuckled. "You're persuasive tonight."

"I'm hungry tonight," she said with a grin. "And curious."

They paused in silence as other guests passed by, heading toward their evening plans. Finally, Sean shrugged.

He smiled slowly, nodding. "Alright. Let's treat ourselves."

"Well, if we're going to argue about a meal, it might as well be over a good one. Let's do it."

"Excellent," she said, looping her arm through his. "I'll make the reservation."

finish with something indulgent?"

They arrived at **Deck 12** just after 7:30 PM, the restaurant glowing with warm ambient lighting and boasting panoramic views of the Norwegian Sea through wide glass windows. The sea shimmered in the darkness beyond, the motion of the ship gentle and rhythmic.

The interior of **Sea & Grass** was intimate and inviting, with dark wood finishes, candlelit tables, and panoramic windows offering views of the gently rippling sea. They were seated at a corner table, cozy and private, with soft instrumental jazz playing in the background.

As soon as their starters arrived, their doubts disappeared. The meal was every bit the indulgence Samantha had hoped for.

They started with **king prawns**, plump and fragrant, sautéed in garlic butter and served with a delicate citrus glaze. Each bite was tender, bursting with briny sweetness and perfectly balanced acidity, lightly grilled with lemon herb butter, served over a delicate fennel salad. The prawns were tender and sweet, the seasoning enhancing without overwhelming.

Samantha closed her eyes briefly. "Okay... I take back everything I said about the price.

Sean nodded, mouth full, and gave a satisfied thumbs-up. "Might be the best prawns I've had in years."

"This is divine," Samantha murmured, savoring each bite.

Sean agreed, wiping the corner of his mouth with a cloth napkin. "I haven't had prawns this good since that trip to Brittany in the '80s."

Next came the **crab soup**, a creamy blend rich with flavor and garnished with delicate herbs and a swirl of smoked paprika oil. The warmth of the dish paired beautifully with the rustic bread served on the side, rich and velvety with just the right touch of spice and cream. They dipped crusty bread into the bowls, lingering over each spoonful.

For their mains, Sean opted for the **grilled sea bass**, starring pan-seared halibut and arctic char, lightly seasoned and resting on a bed of wilted spinach and herb-infused barley. The fish flaked perfectly under their forks, moist and fresh, capturing the essence of the surrounding waters, seasoned with sea salt and dill, resting on a bed of roasted root vegetables and saffron rice. Samantha chose the **Norwegian cod**, perfectly flaky, with a citrus beurre blanc and baby spinach. A side of fresh **salad greens**, tossed in a mild vinaigrette with slivers of radish and shaved Parmesan, balanced the heavier dishes beautifully.

"I can't believe how fresh this tastes," Sean said, dipping a fork into a mound of saffron-scented salad. "They weren't lying on the menu."

"It's like a symphony of flavours," Samantha added. "I'm starting to think we should've come here two nights ago."

"I must admit," Sean said, setting his fork down, "you were right. Worth every penny."

Samantha raised her glass of sparkling water. "To taking chances—and to fresh seafood."

They clinked glasses, the sound delicate and warm, much like the evening itself.

They ended the meal with a light **lemon mousse** and **cloudberry coulis**, the tartness cleansing the palate and leaving them thoroughly satisfied.

As they leaned back in their seats, sipping coffee and watching the moonlight dance on the water, there was a comfortable silence between them—the kind that comes only when people are truly content.

"I'm glad we did this," Sean said.

Samantha smiled. "Me too. Worth every penny."

That night, the excitement continued with the **West End Wonders** live show at the Palladium Theatre. From the moment the curtain rose, Sean and Samantha were swept into a dazzling celebration of musical theatre. The cast performed stirring renditions of songs from *Miss Saigon*, *Hairspray*, *Evita*, and *West Side Story*, their voices powerful and emotive, the choreography electrifying.

"I got goosebumps during *Don't Cry for Me Argentina*," Samantha whispered midway through.

Sean grinned. "I nearly stood up during *America*. That energy— unreal."

The production earned a standing ovation, and both felt elated as they exited the theatre, hearts lifted by the joy of performance and the shared love of music.

"Best show yet," Sean said as they walked slowly back toward the Raffles Bar.

Samantha nodded. "And to think the night's still young."

Following their glowing theatre experience, they made their way to the next lively event onboard—**The Time of Our Lives** gameshow. Held in one of the ship's entertainment lounges, it was a musical and nostalgic journey through the decades. The show whisked the audience back in time to the colorful and iconic eras of the 60s, 70s, 80s, and 90s, complete with costume changes, trivia rounds, and themed music.

Both Sean and Samantha found themselves clapping along, laughing at the contestants' antics, and belting out lyrics to songs they hadn't heard in decades. It was more than entertainment—it was a reminder of all the years they'd lived, danced, and dreamed through. As the show ended, they turned to each other, smiling with shared joy.

"That one really took me back," Sean said.

"To the time of our lives," Samantha replied, raising an imaginary toast.

And with that, they walked into the ship's corridor, the past mingling with the present in the warmth of memory and companionship. They walked slowly back to their cabins, letting the tastes linger in memory and conversation. It had been a day of rich history and even richer flavors, and it was far from over.

Two Solo Together

CHAPTER 7

Under Arctic Skies

Alta, Norway – November 7, 2024

The Ship sailed into Alta, Norway, arriving at 10:00 AM and settling gracefully into the berth as the clouds hovered low and the air hung thick with anticipation. The temperature lingered between 2°C and 6°C, with light rain carried by a moderate breeze. The journey ahead was unlike any of the previous port days—this time, they would stay late into the night. All aboard was scheduled for 1:30 AM, with departure set at 2:00 AM the following morning. The extended stay meant one special opportunity: the chance to witness the Northern Lights from the land of the midnight sun.

Sean and Samantha dressed warmly for the day's chilly and damp weather. Sean wore a black insulated parka, a wool turtleneck sweater, and khaki trousers, with waterproof boots and a fleece-lined beanie. Samantha opted for a forest green parka with a faux-fur trim, thermal leggings under a long wool skirt, a turtleneck, and knee-high waterproof boots. Her knit gloves matched her cranberry-colored scarf, adding a splash of brightness to the grey day.

After a leisurely breakfast at the Borough Market on Deck 12, the couple disembarked with excitement. Complimentary shuttle buses were available for all guests, with the drop-off and pick-up point located at the Tourist Information Centre near Thon Hotel. The bus ride offered them glimpses of Alta's unique Arctic landscape—low-slung houses, snow-dusted rooftops, and a horizon of snow-capped hills.

Their first stop was the Alta Church, its sleek modern architecture striking against the wintery backdrop. Inside, the warm lighting and quiet reverence made for a peaceful start to the day. They moved on to the famous Northern Lights Cathedral, its spiral design inspired by the celestial phenomenon itself. Samantha paused to light a candle and whispered a quiet thought for her grandchildren.

Next, they strolled through the compact but vibrant town center. Samantha was drawn to a small artisan shop featuring hand-knitted goods, Sami crafts, and reindeer leather souvenirs. She browsed slowly, examining each item with the thoughtful eye of a grandmother.

"I think I'll pick up something for the grandkids," she said. "Something warm and handmade."

Sean smiled. "A piece of Norway for them. I think they'd love that."

They visited a local museum showcasing Alta's history—from World War II resistance to the geological wonders of the region—and then walked through the outdoor market, where vendors sold dried fish, berries, and cloudberry preserves. As the rain lightened to a drizzle, they tucked into a cozy café for cups of strong coffee and fresh cinnamon rolls.

As they continued to wander the town, Samantha suggested stopping at a local shop to buy postcards to send back home. Sean picked one with a watercolor painting of the Northern Lights above snow-covered mountains.

"I'll send this to my sister," he said softly.

"You've mentioned her before," Samantha said. "Were you two close?"

"Very. She practically raised me. Our mother worked abroad when I was little. Always traveling, always busy. My sister was only ten years older than me, but she looked after me like a second mother."

Samantha listened with quiet respect as he continued, "She's in a care home now. I think this postcard will bring back memories—she always wanted to see the Northern Lights but never got the chance."

While browsing, Sean bent down to pick up a dropped glove and accidentally knocked his glasses to the ground. One of the nose pads snapped off.

"Oh dear," he muttered, squinting at the frame.

"We'll find a place to fix them," Samantha reassured him.

They asked a nearby shopkeeper for directions and were directed to Specsavers, just a few blocks away. The staff greeted them kindly and inspected Sean's glasses. After a quick adjustment and nose pad replacement, they handed them back with a smile.

"That'll be no charge," the technician said. "It was just a minor fix."

Sean was touched. "Thank you—that's very kind of you."

"Alta's hospitality," Samantha said as they left. "See? Good karma from shopping for the grandkids."

Despite the damp weather, their spirits remained high. The thought of the Northern Lights later that night added a sense of magic to everything they did. They returned to the shuttle stop with bags filled with small treasures and souvenirs, and Samantha clutched a woolen toy she claimed would become her granddaughter's favorite.

As they returned from their afternoon in Alta, the sky began to darken, casting long shadows across the snow-dusted decks. Sean and Samantha dried off from the drizzle and dropped off their shopping bags in their cabins. As they met again to discuss dinner, the thought of a lengthy, formal three-course meal at the Buckingham Restaurant didn't quite appeal.

"We could just go up to Borough Market tonight," Samantha suggested. "A quick buffet, something warm, and we'll be done in half an hour."

Sean nodded. "Makes sense. If the auroras come early, we won't be stuck waiting for dessert while they're dancing overhead."

With a shared smile, they made their way to Deck 12. The Borough Market buffet had comforting smells of roasted meats, stews, and baked vegetables. Sean chose a hearty bowl of beef stew with root vegetables and a side of roasted potatoes, while Samantha picked a lighter plate of grilled salmon, steamed greens, and a warm bread roll. They both topped their meal off with hot apple crumble and custard.

"Quick, cozy, and no tie required," Sean said with satisfaction, leaning back with his coffee.

"And more time for the sky," Samantha added with a wink.

With their appetites satisfied and the night still young, they bundled up and made their way to the upper decks, joining other guests in anticipation of one of nature's greatest shows

They settled in with warm drinks and wrapped themselves in blankets at one of the ship's lounges, watching the fog lift slightly as night approached. The ship's crew had organized Northern Lights watch stations on Deck 14 and announcements would be made if the lights became visible.

Samantha leaned toward Sean. "Do you think we'll see them tonight?"

"I think... if we're lucky, and we stay up late enough, we just might," he said.

And so they waited, hopeful under Arctic skies.

As twilight descended over Alta, an early darkness cloaked the town in a velvety hush. By 4:00 PM, the sun had dipped below the horizon, casting a silvery-blue hue across the landscape. A thin fog curled along the waterfront, but patches of clear sky gradually opened above them. The temperature held steady around 3°C, and guests returned to the ship to warm up and prepare for the long, expectant night.

After dinner, Sean and Samantha found a quiet corner near the open deck on level 14. Wrapped in thick scarves and holding steaming mugs of hot chocolate, they sat side by side on deck chairs, their gazes fixed on the darkened sky. Around them, a quiet crowd had gathered — passengers speaking in hushed tones, pointing their phones skyward, waiting. More people rushed to Deck 14 where other passengers had already gathered with hot drinks, cameras, and eyes turned skyward. The clouds had finally thinned, revealing the stars — and something else.

By 9:00 PM, the sky above Alta grew darker. And then, once again, the show began. **Ribbons of green light danced and waved** above them, followed by sudden bursts of **blue and violet**. Then came a swirl of **crimson and pink**, gently pulsing across the northern horizon. The lights appeared **every one to two minutes**, each time more vivid, more dramatic, and more surreal.

Then, just before 9:30 PM, as the ship gently rocked in the quiet harbor, a buzz moved through the corridors—"They're here!" a ripple of gasps and murmurs swept across the deck. A faint green shimmer appeared, like a soft watercolor stroke, slowly unfurling across the northern horizon. The glow intensified, swirling into waves of emerald and hints of violet. Curtains of light danced gracefully in the sky, rippling and pulsing as if set to music only the stars could hear.

Sean leaned forward, eyes wide. "There they are."

Samantha clutched his arm. "Oh, my goodness... it's more beautiful than I imagined."

It began as a green ribbon, stretching like a brushstroke across the inky black canvas above. Then, almost as if on cue, **the sky erupted in waves of emerald, crimson, soft pink, and deep indigo**, moving and shifting in slow, elegant patterns.

Every one or two minutes, **new bursts of color appeared**—cascading and dancing, as if the heavens were putting on a private ballet. The lights shimmered over the darkened mountains and reflected in the calm water below.

Sean's eyes widened, and his breath caught. "I've never seen anything like this in my life."

Samantha, with her hands clasped in front of her chest, whispered, "It's like the sky is breathing."

They stood side by side, silent for a long while, both moved beyond words. Around them, people gasped, cheered quietly, and pointed as the auroras swirled and shifted with hypnotic rhythm.

"I'm so glad we didn't sit down for a long dinner," Sean said with a grin, his voice barely audible over the soft awe of the crowd.

Samantha nodded. "Nothing would've been as filling as this."

Neither spoke for a long moment. They simply watched—awed, humbled, and a little emotional. The auroras flickered like celestial dancers, and even the crisp Arctic wind seemed to pause in reverence.

Time lost meaning as the phenomenon continued. People gasped, cheered quietly, and stood shoulder to shoulder on the observation deck. Sean's eyes welled up—not just from the cold—and Samantha clasped his arm, resting her head lightly against his shoulder.

"We're going to remember this night forever," she whispered.

Samantha broke the silence softly. "I feel like the universe is smiling tonight."

Sean nodded. "And letting us be a part of it."

The two leaned against the railing, their shoulders brushing, the cold forgotten in the glow of something eternal and rare. For those few magical hours, **the Arctic sky painted memories that would last the rest of their lives**.

They stayed on deck until nearly midnight, marveling at the cosmic display. It was cold, yes—but the kind of cold you didn't mind when your heart felt so warm.

They stayed out until **2:00 AM**, long after most passengers had gone to bed. As the **ship slowly departed Alta**, pushing away from the dock under the painted sky, the waves shimmered with reflections of emerald and rose. The engines rumbled softly beneath their feet.

Even after returning to their cabins, sleep did not come easily. The **excitement of witnessing such a rare and mesmerizing display** kept their minds alive with images and wonder. Every time they closed their eyes, they saw the sky again—the colors, the motion, the silence broken only by the sea.

It had been a perfect night under the Arctic heavens.

CHAPTER 8

Change of Course

Tromsø, Norway – November 8, 2024

The Ship made her way into Tromsø, arriving at 11:00 AM under a heavy sky and was scheduled to depart at 9 PM. The temperature ranged from 5°C to 10°C, with occasional drizzle and a gentle breeze rolling over the fjords. The berth was Breivika Number 3, and it was a last-minute change from the originally scheduled stop at Leknes, Lofoten Islands. The Captain's voice over the intercom earlier that morning had explained that due to an unfavorable forecast—strong winds up to 47 knots and waves reaching 8 meters—the tender operations at Leknes were deemed unsafe. Safety always came first, and so, Tromsø became their new Arctic destination.

Sean and Samantha had slept in after their late night under the Northern Lights in Alta. By the time they got up, it was too late for breakfast alone, so they opted for a combined breakfast and lunch at the Borough Market on Deck 12. The casual buffet offered a comforting variety—scrambled eggs, smoked salmon, grilled sausages, and warm pastries, followed by fresh salads and a pasta bar. They ate leisurely, sipping hot tea and chatting about their plans for the day.

After their meal, they made their way to the gangway, ensuring they had their cruise cards for reboarding. A complimentary shuttle bus service provided by the port authority awaited them. The drop-off and pick-up point was conveniently located near the Radisson Blu Hotel in the city center, with buses operating regularly throughout the day.

Despite the grey skies, the city welcomed the guests with its charming blend of modern living and Arctic culture. Sean and Samantha took their time disembarking, wrapped in cozy layers. Sean wore his trusted parka, this time with a thick knit jumper and denim jeans, while Samantha opted for a puffer coat over a sweater dress with fleece-lined leggings and her favorite wool boots. The dress code for the day was casual, which suited their exploratory spirit.

They began their visit with a trip to the iconic Arctic Cathedral, its angular white design standing stark against the dark hillside.

Inside, shafts of soft natural light filtered through the striking stained-glass windows. Afterwards, they wandered the cobbled streets of the city center, where a small weekend market was in full swing—locals selling cloudberry jams, knitted mittens, and dried cod.

Tromsø's museums drew them in next, particularly the Polar Museum, where they marveled at stories of Arctic explorers and the harsh realities of life in the polar regions. They stopped by a maritime exhibit and admired relics from centuries-old seafaring expeditions.

A cozy coffee shop near the harbor provided them shelter from a sudden drizzle. They sat with mugs of rich hot chocolate and watched the people of Tromsø go about their day. Samantha couldn't resist a bit of shopping—she found a woolen hat for her grandson and some decorative candles made from Arctic herbs.

"It's strange to think we might have been bouncing on waves in Leknes," Sean commented.

"Instead, we're safe and snug here, with candles and coffee," Samantha replied, smiling. "Not a bad trade."

As they relaxed, Samantha turned to Sean with an idea. "You know, I saw on the excursion list that there's a 'War Time in Trondheim' tour coming up. It sounds fascinating—stories of occupation, resistance, life during the war. I think I'd like to go."

Sean nodded thoughtfully. "Sounds serious. But interesting. Let's check the details when we're back onboard."

"It just makes me think," Samantha continued, "how different life was back then. What people had to endure. I'd like to understand it more."

"It's a good idea," Sean agreed. "And we'll still have time to explore more together, no doubt."

"It's not about doing everything together," Samantha said gently. "It's about enjoying what matters and sharing what we learn."

Their day in Tromsø was a peaceful one, filled with discovery and comfort despite the cold. The last shuttle back to the ship left just before 8:00 PM, ensuring that all guests were aboard by the 9:00 PM departure. The lights of Tromsø twinkled as the ship pulled away, a reflection of the quiet beauty they had found in the Arctic city.

With thoughts of Northern lights still fresh from the previous night in Alta, they headed back inside, ready for the next chapter in their journey.

That evening, they dressed for dinner and returned to the Buckingham Restaurant on Deck 7. The menu offered a delicious array of options. Sean and Samantha both chose the soup of the day to start, followed by duck for Sean and chicken pasta for Samantha. They shared a fruit plate and indulged in a rich chocolate dessert, complemented by cups of tea and coffee. A glass of red wine rounded off the meal beautifully, and they enjoyed the elegant atmosphere and warm service as they reflected on the day's highlights.

They returned to the ship just in time to relax before dinner. Tonight's dinner was at the Buckingham Restaurant on Deck 7. The menu was rich and satisfying: duck and chicken mains, soup of the day, pasta, and a selection of desserts including chocolate confections and fresh fruit plates. They enjoyed tea and coffee after the meal, and shared a bottle of red wine.

The dress code for the evening was casual. Sean chose a comfortable yet neat pair of dark slacks and a light navy sweater over a collared shirt, while Samatha wore her favorite patterned blouse with tailored black trousers and a cozy shawl, perfect for a relaxed yet elegant look. They felt at ease in the welcoming ambiance of the dining room, surrounded by fellow guests also dressed comfortably yet appropriately for the evening's tone.

As the evening settled in, Samantha brought up more thoughts about the upcoming visit to Trondheim. "I've been reading up," she said, showing Sean a brochure she picked up from the excursion desk. "Did you know Trondheim was the capital of Norway during the Viking Age? And that Nidaros Cathedral is one of the most important pilgrimage sites in Northern Europe?"

Sean looked intrigued. "I didn't. Sounds like there's a lot to take in. Churches, cathedrals, war history, markets. I imagine it's going to be a special stop."

"Exactly," she said. "There's also the Archbishop's Palace, and the open-air folk museum. Not to mention the charming wooden houses along the old wharves by the Nidelva River. I think it might be my favorite port."

"I'm starting to feel the same," Sean replied with a smile. "Let's make the most of it."

Later in the evening, as they strolled through the ship, Sean and Samatha stopped in front of the Triple 7 Casino. A vibrant energy flowed out from the open doors — the sounds of slot machines, laughter, and the shuffle of cards filled the air. They paused to look inside. The Blackjack tables intrigued them.

"I've never played Blackjack before," Sean admitted, peering in with a curious smile.

"Me neither," Samatha replied, laughing softly. "Do you think it's too late to learn?"

"Might be fun to try," he mused. "Even if we lose a few pounds, it's all in good fun."

They agreed to return another night after reading up on the rules. For now, they watched from the sidelines, enjoying the buzz and considering whether they'd become late-night high-rollers — or at least, adventurous beginners.

As the evening continued, they made their way to the Palladium Theatre for the night's headline show: Emily Haig. A powerhouse soprano, Emily dazzled the audience with her commanding stage presence, dramatic flair, and stunning vocals. Her repertoire blended classical elegance with contemporary power — transitioning effortlessly from Evanescence's haunting melodies to the passionate arias of Bizet, and even crooning a touch of Michael Bublé.

The audience was enthralled, and Sean and Samatha sat captivated, exchanging smiles during the standing ovation. The mix of raw talent, stylish performance, and genre-spanning setlist made it a night to remember — another magical moment on their unforgettable journey.

After the theatre show, they made their way to the Centre Court to enjoy Joe's Laid Back Cabaret. The relaxed atmosphere and smooth music were a perfect contrast to the grandeur of the earlier performance. Joe's charm and easygoing style made the guests feel like they were among friends, as he sang a medley of classics and chatted between songs. Sean and Samatha smiled, swaying slightly in their seats, relishing yet another lovely evening at sea.

As they walked back toward their cabins, they stopped to admire the ship's glistening holiday decor. Samatha pointed at a small poster displayed on an information board near the elevators.

"Look, a future cruise offer," she said, tapping it. "10% off if we book a Christmas cruise to the Canaries."

Sean leaned in. "Hmm... Christmas in the sun? That does sound tempting."

"And warm," she added. "Much warmer than here!"

He chuckled. "I could get used to swapping jumpers for short sleeves and sunhats."

Samatha nodded, her eyes twinkling. "Imagine sipping a cocktail on deck while watching the Atlantic waves — instead of huddling in layers."

"Should we go talk to the cruise consultant tomorrow?" Sean asked. "At least to get the details."

"Definitely," Samatha smiled. "It would be something to look forward to after this magical trip ends."

They continued down the corridor, chatting about potential excursions, holiday meals, and sunny beaches — already dreaming of their next sea-bound adventure.

Finally, after such a long and eventful day, they returned to their cabin just after midnight. Exhausted but content, they slipped under the covers, still glowing from the evening's delights. With the gentle rocking of the ship and dreams of Northern lights and sunny holidays ahead, they soon drifted off into a deep, happy sleep.

CHAPTER 9

Change of Course

At Sea Tromsø, Norway – November 9, 2024

The Ship ship remained docked overnight in **Tromsø, Norway**, its towering white hull glowing softly under the city's lights. The stillness of the port in the early morning was broken only by the quiet hum of machinery and the low chatter of activity on the quay.

The day began early for Sean and Samatha. After an unforgettable day exploring Tromsø and a restful night aboard, they awoke to the gentle hum of port activity outside their cabin window. The ship was still berthed at **Breivika Number 3**, Tromsø, having stayed overnight — a rare occurrence on their cruise journey.

Through the misty glass, they watched the bustle on the pier as **new cruise staff boarded the ship** and several **existing crew members disembarked**, waving to their colleagues. There was something deeply human in that exchange — the quiet rhythm of transitions, of people coming and going, of lives intersecting briefly in this floating community. **All new cruise staff** were boarding the ship with luggage in tow, fresh-faced and full of anticipation. At the same time, **some crew members disembarked**, their contracts completed, waving goodbye to friends made during months at sea.

The temperature outside was **3–6°C**, a **light rain** falling with a **fresh breeze** brushing over the decks. There was something contemplative about this morning — a quiet changeover, the passing of torches behind the scenes. The sky remained a thick grey, typical for northern Norway in late autumn, but it didn't dampen the sense of something special about the day.

The ship schdule to depart **9:00 AM**, the entire day was designated as a **sea day,** allowing passengers to unwind and enjoy onboard activities while sailing further along the northern coast of Norway. A time for guests to relax, recharge, and enjoy the ship's amenities before continuing their Arctic voyage.

Unlike their usual slow starts, **Sean and Samatha woke early**, stirred by the subtle commotion of the port and a renewed sense of curiosity. Wanting to try something different, they decided to **have breakfast at Restaurant** — their **first time** dining there in the morning. Breaking from their usual habit of buffet breakfasts, Sean and Samatha decided to try something different — a proper **sit-down breakfast at the Buckingham Restaurant** on Deck 7, their first time there for the morning meal.

As they entered, they were greeted with the elegant hush of fine china, soft music, and the wafting aroma of freshly brewed coffee and buttery croissants. A window seat gave them a final glimpse of Tromsø as the city faded into the morning mist.

It was an elegant change of pace. Seated at a crisp white-clothed table near a wide window, they ordered from a small but carefully crafted menu. Sean opted for a full English breakfast — sausages, grilled tomato, eggs, black pudding, mushrooms, and toast — served with strong coffee and a side of orange juice. Samatha chose smoked salmon and scrambled eggs on toast with a small bowl of fresh berries and a pot of Earl Grey tea.

"Why didn't we come here before?" Samatha asked, dabbing her lips with a napkin.

"I know," Sean replied, cutting into his sausage. "It's a whole different experience from the buffet. Feels a bit more... indulgent."

As the ship pulled away from the **Breivika Pier**, they watched Tromsø shrink into the distance. The fjords framed the city with dramatic cliffs and snowy caps, and for a brief moment, the clouds parted to reveal a golden glow on the horizon.

Today's sea day promised to be relaxing — but also reflective, as the cruise passed its midpoint. There were still new sights ahead, but the journey thus far had already brought more than either of them expected.

The service was warm, unhurried, and the quiet ambiance felt luxurious. impeccable, a graceful dance of waiters and waitresses anticipating every need. They both agreed it was a lovely change from the bustling buffet and decided they'd return before the cruise ended.

"I think this might be our new breakfast ritual," Sean said with a grin, buttering a croissant.

"Only if you promise not to steal my berries next time," Samatha teased.

After breakfast, they strolled through the ship, enjoying the calm of the mid-morning hours. They paused briefly on the promenade deck, braving the drizzle under their umbrellas. The town of Tromsø looked still and peaceful from afar — snow-dusted hillsides, red and yellow buildings, and a long bridge stretching across the icy water.

The announcement came over the PA system, detailing the day's activities: art classes, Nordic lectures, culinary demos, and another thrilling theatre production in the evening.

They exchanged smiles, knowing they'd find a few moments to themselves too — but for now, it was time to see what this sea day would bring.

Later in the day, they signed up for the "Master Art of Cocktail Making" session. Sean was eager and thought it was a great deal — five exotic drinks to sample while learning professional techniques. "It's not every day you get to shake cocktails with the pros," he grinned. Samatha, however, was more hesitant. "You know I'm not really a drinker," she said, raising an eyebrow as Sean gave her a playful nudge. Still, she decided to join for the experience and enjoyed watching the creativity and flair involved, sipping lightly on a fruity mocktail.

Samatha also spent some quiet time at the onboard salon, treating herself to a luxury pedicure and reflexology foot massage. The experience left her feeling pampered and rejuvenated. "It was absolutely divine," she said afterward. "The therapist was gentle and skilled, and I feel like I'm walking on clouds now."

Meanwhile, Sean went shopping at the Galleria spread across decks 5, 6, and 7. He was particularly interested in designer watches. As he browsed brands like Citizen, Tissot, Fossil, Timex, Anne Klein, and Sekonda, he found it difficult to choose. "They're all duty-free, which makes it even more tempting," he told Samatha later. He held up two options for her opinion, and they enjoyed a playful debate over which looked better on his wrist.

For lunch, they returned to Borough Market for something lighter — smoked salmon sandwiches, lentil soup, and a shared plate of apple crumble. They enjoyed their meal at a table by the windows, watching as the light rain turned to sleet and back again.

As evening approached, the ship gently cruised away from Tromsø under the darkening sky. Tonight's dress code was *smart*, and Sean and Samatha took extra care in preparing for their evening.

Sean selected a charcoal grey blazer over a crisp white shirt, paired with navy chinos and polished oxford shoes. He debated adding a tie but decided against it for a more relaxed elegance. Samatha wore a navy blue cocktail dress with a soft shimmer to the fabric, complemented by a delicate silver necklace and matching earrings. She draped a light cream wrap over her shoulders to ward off the evening chill.

"You look stunning," Sean said, offering his arm as they left their cabin.

"And you look very dashing," Samatha replied, her eyes twinkling.

They arrived at the Buckingham Restaurant just after 7 PM. The ambiance was warm, the lighting soft, and the staff greeted them with friendly smiles and a gentle nod of recognition. They were seated near the window, where they could watch the distant fjords slowly slipping by.

The three-course meal was beautifully presented. For starters, Sean chose a leek and potato soup, while Samatha enjoyed a smoked trout salad with dill cream. Their mains included a perfectly cooked lamb rump for Sean and a delicate poached sole with lemon butter sauce for Samatha. They shared a plate of roast vegetables and seasoned couscous on the side.

Over dinner that evening, Sean shared his experience from earlier in the day when he had joined the crew's behind-the-scenes excursion. "It was incredible," he began, eyes lighting up. "I got to see the sound and light booth in the theatre, and they even took us backstage. The mooring deck was a real eye-opener—massive ropes and all the heavy machinery that keeps this ship in place."

Samatha listened intently as he continued, "We visited the chef's table, which is actually part of the main galley—it was spotless, like a dance of coordination and cleanliness. Then we went to the provision area, photo lab, and even the main laundry. But the highlight? The Bridge. Watching the officers monitor all the ship's systems was fascinating. It's like a calm, high-tech command center."

"Sounds like you really enjoyed it," Samatha smiled. "I would've liked to see the chef's table. Maybe next time."

For dessert, Sean couldn't resist the sticky toffee pudding, and Samatha opted for the vanilla panna cotta with a berry compote. They sipped on glasses of Cabernet Sauvignon and ended their meal with a rich espresso for Sean and mint tea for Samatha.

"Smart night suits us," Sean said, raising his glass.

"To us, and to nights like these," Samatha replied, clinking gently.

After dinner, they headed to the theatre to enjoy a live band performance titled "Mersey Beats: The Music Story of Liverpool." The show was a joyful celebration of the city's musical legacy, packed with energetic renditions of classics from The Beatles, Gerry and the Pacemakers, and other iconic Merseybeat bands. Sean tapped his feet enthusiastically, while Samatha swayed to the rhythm, both utterly immersed in the vibrant, nostalgic atmosphere.

After the concert, they made their way back to the Palladium Theatre for the much-anticipated performance of "Dance Dance Dance," choreographed by none other than Strictly's Anton Du Beke. With guest virtual appearances and an exciting world tour of the best dance styles, the show dazzled with sequences ranging from fiery Latin numbers to elegant ballroom routines. The lighting, the footwork, the music—it was a thrilling tribute to dance through the ages. Sean and Samatha clapped along, captivated by the energy and precision on stage.

As the night matured, Sean and Samatha made their way up to the Observatory Lounge where the late-night disco was in full swing. The dance floor was designed like a spaceship, complete with futuristic lighting and pulsating beats curated by DJ Power. They couldn't resist the infectious rhythm. Hand in hand, they danced beneath starlit projections and mirrored lights, laughing and spinning to classic dance hits and modern beats.

"I haven't danced like this in years," Samatha said breathlessly.

"Me neither," Sean replied, grinning as the bass dropped. "But it feels fantastic."

They stayed until well past midnight, enjoying every moment, before finally heading back to their cabin, their hearts light with joy and their feet delightfully sore from a night well danced.

They talked about their plans for the next port, wondering what new sights and experiences awaited. As the ship sailed through the cold night, Sean and Samatha reflected on how far they'd come — both geographically and emotionally — since the cruise began.

Their bond had grown deeper with every shared moment: from dancing under the Northern Lights to laughing at sea-themed trivia, from planning future holidays to simply sitting in peaceful silence.

Eventually, they made their way back to their cabin, with the night sky glittering above. Another perfect day behind them, and more adventures just over the horizon.

Back in her solo cabin, Samatha lay in bed staring at the ceiling. She smiled to herself, heart warm with emotion. The fun they had — dancing, laughing, teasing — made her feel like a teenager again, full of excitement and wonder. In the neighboring cabin, Sean was already asleep, a soft smile resting on his face as he dreamed sweetly of his youth, reliving moments that made him feel alive and young once more.

The night settled around them gently, wrapping both in a peaceful cocoon of memories, connection, and anticipation for the days still ahead.

Two Solo Together

CHAPTER 10

Change of Course

Narvik, Norway – November 10, 2024

The Ship ship arrived at Narvik, Norway, at precisely 8 AM. The clouds hung low in the sky, a gentle drizzle misting the air and softening the views of the snow-dusted mountains beyond the town. The temperature hovered between 5 to 7°C, with a light wind blowing from the fjord. Sunrise had come at 8:47 AM, but with sunset due as early as 2:19 PM, the day already felt fleeting.

Docked at Pier 3 Quay, the ship was nestled comfortably in the harbor. Complimentary shuttle buses were available, but only for guests with limited mobility. For Sean and Samatha, who both felt invigorated from the previous night's dancing, walking into Narvik town seemed ideal.

That morning, they had a quiet breakfast together at the Borough Market. The usual lively chatter was subdued as many passengers were preparing for short excursions, given the limited time in port. Sean and Samatha enjoyed their meal in a relaxed silence, sipping warm tea and sharing a light plate of pastries and fruit. They both knew their excursions were scheduled soon and didn't want to rush.

Bundled in warm jackets, gloves, and scarves, they stepped off the ship and onto Norwegian soil once more. Narvik had a charm of its own — quiet, rugged, and steeped in history. They wandered together through winding streets, past quaint shops and local cafés, eventually reaching the town's church. The air inside the church was warm and filled with the scent of candles and polished wood, offering a peaceful moment of reflection.

Next, they explored a small outdoor market with handcrafted goods and local delicacies, before stepping into the War Museum, where Samatha lingered over photographs from World War II. She spoke softly about how her father used to tell stories about the war, and Sean listened, touched by her memories.

Later, they stopped by a local café near the museum, sipping hot chocolate and sharing a cinnamon bun. From their window seat, they watched townsfolk go about their routines, a gentle calm filling their hearts.

"You know," Sean said, looking out, "this town feels like a secret whispered by the mountains."

Samatha smiled. "It really does. Quiet, but full of stories."

In the afternoon, Sean went on an excursion to the Polar Wildlife Park, the northernmost animal park in the world. He was amazed by the variety of Arctic animals, including lynx, wolverines, reindeer, Arctic foxes, and even wolves. Guided by a local ranger, he learned about their natural habitats and conservation efforts. Sean especially enjoyed watching the majestic brown bears, lumbering through their enclosures in the cold mist.

Meanwhile, Samatha chose a different cultural path and went on the Isogaisa Sami Experience. She was warmly welcomed into a lavvu—a traditional Sami tent—and listened to stories of the indigenous Sami people, their ancient way of life, and deep connection to the natural world. She experienced joik singing, sampled traditional Sami food, and learned about reindeer herding. The ceremony and storytelling left a profound impression on her, and she left feeling both grounded and inspired.

By the time the golden light of the short Arctic afternoon began to fade, they headed back toward the harbor, arm in arm, sharing stories from their separate adventures and enjoying the last glimpses of Narvik's charm before returning to the ship before the 6 PM departure.

Once back onboard, they decided to unwind at the Consulate Bar on Deck 10. Nestled into one of the cozy corners with a view of the still harbor, they ordered warm drinks—Sean chose an Irish coffee, while Samatha enjoyed a hot spiced apple cider. The soft jazz music in the background made the perfect atmosphere to exchange thoughts.

"Those Arctic foxes were something else," Sean said, shaking his head in amazement. "You could see the intelligence in their eyes."

Samatha smiled. "The Sami people... they speak with such reverence about the land and the animals. I feel like I was given a glimpse into a world I've never known."

They compared notes on their excursions, each fascinated by the other's experience. Sean showed her a few photos he'd managed to snap of the reindeer, and Samatha described the gentle rhythm of the joik singing, even humming a few notes for him.

"That song... it stays with you," she said.

"Just like this place," Sean added, looking out the window at the misty coastline. "Quiet. Majestic."

As they continued to talk, other passengers in the bar overheard their conversation. A woman named Anne, aged 57, approached with her elderly aunt, who was around 82. They had just returned from their own excursions and were eager to share.

"We heard you visited the Sami experience and the wildlife park," Anne said warmly. "We went on the Scenic Fjord Drive and the Exclusive Arctic Train Adventure. Quite a contrast, I suppose!"

Samatha and Sean welcomed them to the conversation. Anne described the breathtaking fjord views, icy-blue waters nestled between towering cliffs, and the soothing rhythm of the train as it glided through the Arctic wilderness.

Her aunt added with a gleam in her eye, "The train conductor even told us stories from his childhood here. I felt like I was stepping back in time."

They all laughed, sipped their drinks, and continued to exchange impressions well into the early evening. Despite their varied experiences, they all agreed that Narvik had quietly left its mark on them—a town of small wonders, rich culture, and tranquil beauty.

Her aunt added with a gleam in her eye, "The train conductor even told us stories from his childhood here. I felt like I was stepping back in time."

As the four of them sat together, the conversation flowed naturally. Anne and her aunt, Jane, shared that they were originally from the Philippines but had lived and worked in San Francisco, USA, for more than forty years. Their eyes sparkled with travel tales from across Asia, Europe, and the Americas.

Samatha was especially interested in their stories about island life in the Philippines, and Jane spoke warmly of her youth by the sea. Sean asked about their experiences traveling as a family, and Anne explained how she had always brought her aunt along on cruises since retiring.

"Travel keeps you young," Jane said with a wink. "And cruising is the perfect way to enjoy the world—without packing and unpacking every other day."

They exchanged opinions on the best destinations they'd visited, from the canals of Venice to the cherry blossoms in Kyoto. It was one of those conversations where time disappeared, bound by shared passions and mutual curiosity.

When the ship finally prepared to leave Narvik, the group promised to meet again later on the cruise. As they waved goodbye, there was a quiet joy in the connection they'd made—fellow wanderers, brought together by chance, sharing stories under the Arctic sky.

Samatha and Sean stayed in the bar a little longer, as the ship slowly made its way away from Narvik and into the Arctic waters once again, Sean and Samatha lingered a little longer in their cozy corner. The soft glow of the ship's lights flickered across their faces as the topic turned more personal.

Samatha took a long sip of her cider and looked into her cup for a moment. "Sean," she began softly, "I haven't told many people this... but I've been married twice."

Sean looked at her gently, listening without interruption.

"My first marriage... it wasn't great. We were too young, maybe, or just too different. It ended after a few years. We divorced peacefully, but I carried the weight of disappointment for a long time."

She paused, and Sean placed his hand lightly on hers.

"And then," she continued, "I met Daniel. He was an American pilot. Confident, kind, always smiling. We were married for six years. He showed me the world from the skies... until one day, his plane had a technical failure." Her voice faltered slightly. "It caught fire in the air. They never made it back. It was more than ten years ago."

Sean gave her hand a gentle squeeze. "I'm so sorry, Samatha."

She nodded slowly, tears barely glistening in her eyes. "I don't talk about it much. But... sometimes it helps. Especially when I meet someone who listens."

"You're not alone," Sean said quietly. "And it's okay to still carry those memories. They're part of what made you who you are."

They sat in silence for a while, their hands still entwined, the hum of the ship and soft music around them like a gentle embrace. In that moment, beneath the northern skies, two hearts quietly connected—each carrying their past, and somehow, beginning to share a little more of the future.

Then, Sean gently smiled and said, "Would it be alright if I shared a little of my story too?"

Samatha nodded, her expression tender.

"I was married once," Sean began. "For forty years. Her name was Margaret. I met her in sixth form—my school was all boys, hers was all girls. We first talked at a joint school dance, and something just clicked."

He chuckled softly. "We ended up going to the same university. I proposed to her just after graduation, and we got married not long after. We had two kids—a boy and a girl. They're all grown up now, with families of their own."

"Do you see them often?" Samatha asked.

"I try to," he replied. "They're busy people, you know. Careers, kids. But we're close. And I'm lucky to have seven wonderful grandchildren. They keep me on my toes, even from a distance."

He looked away for a moment, his eyes misting. "Margaret passed five years ago. Cancer. It was quick. Too quick."

Samatha reached for his hand. "She sounds like she was amazing."

Sean nodded. "She was. And though she's gone, I still feel her presence sometimes. Especially when I'm watching a sunset, or hearing a song she loved. But being here now, with you... it feels good to talk about her. Like she's part of the journey too."

There was a soft pause, filled with mutual understanding.

"Thank you for sharing that with me, Sean," Samatha said.

He looked at her and smiled, a warmth behind his eyes. "Thank you for listening."

And with that, they sat together as the Arctic night surrounded them, two kindred spirits who had weathered storms of their own, finding comfort in shared stories and the quiet promise of new beginnings.

And with that, they sat together as the Arctic night surrounded them, two kindred spirits who had weathered storms of their own, finding comfort in shared stories and the quiet promise of new beginnings.

Outside the window, Narvik had long disappeared into the mist. The sea stretched out like a sheet of midnight silk, undisturbed and serene. Somewhere above the clouds, the northern lights were rumored to dance, though the weather held them shy tonight. Still, the gentle rhythm of the ship and the warmth between them was enough.

Eventually, Samatha leaned her head against Sean's shoulder. "I think I needed this trip more than I realized," she whispered.

"So did I," Sean replied, wrapping an arm around her. "More than I knew."

They sat that way a while longer, until the bar began to empty and the soft jazz faded into quiet. Together, they returned to their stateroom, hand in hand, the hallway hushed, the ship gliding steadily toward open sea.

Later that evening, Sean noticed the ship's daily programme had listed a special Remember Sunday Service, held by Marian in the Palladium Lounge. The announcement said it was to honour those lost in conflicts past and present, and open to veterans and all guests who wished to attend.

Samatha told Sean she would like to go.

At the service, the room was still and reverent. Veterans and guests, some wearing medals, gathered quietly. Samatha stood among them. A hush fell as Marian led a short, heartfelt tribute. A poem was read, and then the room fell into a solemn, powerful silence for two minutes.

Samatha closed her eyes during the silence, her thoughts drifting to Daniel, and the life they might have continued together. Sean stood at the back, watching her with respect and understanding. He too remembered Margaret and all the memories they'd shared.

As the final notes of the trumpet echoed softly through the Palladium, there was a sense of unity in grief, remembrance, and gratitude. Samatha wiped away a single tear as she turned and saw Sean waiting, his eyes kind and steady.

In that moment, they both felt that though the past may be filled with loss, the present still held hope, and companionship made all the difference.

After the service, as they walked slowly back through the softly lit corridor, Sean gently said, "Let's have dinner at the Buckingham Restaurant tonight. Something warm, something comforting."

Samatha nodded. "I'd like that."

Over dinner, they shared a quiet table, enjoying a well-prepared meal and soft conversation. Then Sean smiled and said, "After this... how about we go to the Palladium again?"

"Oh? Another concert?" Samatha asked.

"Not quite. It's a comedy night. David Huband is performing."

Samatha raised a brow. "Comedy?"

"I think we could use a good laugh," Sean said. "You know... laugh our hearts out, forget our troubles, get happy, and chase all the blues away."

Samatha smiled warmly. "That sounds perfect."

And so they did—ending their night in a theatre filled with laughter, holding hands in the dark as David Huband brought joy and levity to their hearts.

Together, they laughed again. Not just at the jokes—but for life, for memories, for hope. And it was enough.

They left the lounge together in silence, the quiet between them rich with understanding. Outside, the ship moved steadily through the dark Arctic waters, stars peeking through breaks in the clouds above.

Back in Sean's cabin, Samatha stood by the balcony window, watching the snowy peaks fade into the night. Sean joined her, wrapping an arm around her shoulder. They stood like that for a long while, saying nothing, simply sharing the view—and the comfort of each other's presence.

As they finally turned in for the night, the warmth of their shared stories lingered between them like a soft light in the dark. Sleep came gently, and with it, the peace of knowing that even amidst the chill of the northern world, hearts could still find warmth again.

With the dim light casting a golden hue across the room, what tomorrow might bring, about how strange and beautiful it was to feel so seen. And when sleep finally came, it was peaceful and deep.

Somewhere ahead, —another place to explore, another story to unfold.

Two Solo Together

CHAPTER 11

Change of Course

Bodø, Norway – November 11, 2024

The Ship ship arrived in Bodø, Norway, right on schedule at 8:00 AM. The grey skies hung low with light rain, and a gentle breeze rolled in from the coast. The temperature rested between 6 to 7°C, and while not freezing, the air was crisp enough to keep jackets zipped and scarves wrapped tightly. Today's gangway was located on Deck 7—an unusual shift from the typical Deck 5—and this small change sparked a bit of curiosity among passengers.

Sean and Samatha met at their usual spot in the lounge just after breakfast. Over steaming cups of tea, they reviewed the day's excursion options with excitement and deliberation.

"The Lofoten Island flightseeing tour sounds incredible," Sean said, tapping the brochure with interest. "But it's weather-dependent. Clouds might ruin the views."

Samatha nodded. "I saw that too. And there's the Saltstraumen Maelstrom boat ride. But it sounds a bit intense—might be too rough in this weather."

"Then there's the Bodø Cathedral and Aviation Museum combo," Sean added. "It's less risky with the rain. I've read the museum has one of the best aviation collections in Europe."

Samatha tilted her head thoughtfully. "Hmm. I do like the sound of that. But I was also tempted by the Kjerringøy Trading Post—so much history and old Norwegian charm."

They agreed to part ways for the afternoon again—Sean would go on the RIB boat excursion to Saltstraumen, while Samatha would choose the land-based tour to discover the natural wonders of Saltstraumen.

Before their excursions, they decided to take a morning walk through the town together, since the gangway had opened earlier than expected.

Bundled up in waterproof jackets, they stepped off the ship and onto the slick, rain-kissed pavement of the port. The town of Bodø greeted them with understated Nordic charm—modest buildings with painted facades, quiet streets lined with bicycles, and friendly locals bustling about under umbrellas. The walk to the town center was short and pleasant, passing by art installations, cozy coffee houses, and modern shops.

They stopped briefly at a local bakery, drawn in by the scent of fresh cardamom buns. Sharing a warm pastry and sipping coffee, they sat by the window and watched the drizzle blur the town's gentle lines.

"There's something soothing about this place," Samatha said quietly.

Sean nodded. "It's the kind of calm that seeps into your bones."

As the rain continued to fall softly on the glass, they readied themselves for their respective excursions, both looking forward to exploring more of this hidden gem in the north of Norway.

After their relaxing stroll, they parted ways. Sean suited up in a waterproof drysuit and boarded the fast-moving RIB boat with a small group. The journey to Saltstraumen was exhilarating—waves splashing, wind whipping past, and the pulse of the engine vibrating through his seat. Once there, he witnessed the extraordinary whirlpools created by the world's strongest tidal current. It was a breathtaking display of nature's raw power.

Meanwhile, Samatha's excursion offered a quieter yet equally captivating experience. She walked along scenic trails that led to panoramic viewpoints, marveling at the power and mystery of Saltstraumen from the land. Her guide explained the history, geology, and folklore of the area. She took photos of the swirling waters below and even spotted a pair of sea eagles soaring overhead.

By late afternoon, they returned to the ship and reunited at the Botanical Lounge on Deck 10. With warm drinks in hand, they sank into plush armchairs and began comparing notes.

"You should have seen the whirlpools up close," Sean said with bright eyes. "It's like nature flexing its muscles."

Samatha smiled. "And you should have seen them from above. It's humbling. The land tells its own story, you know?"

They laughed and chatted, both enriched by their different experiences, feeling grateful once again for this journey they were sharing.

While relaxing at the bar, they spotted their friends Ann and Jane approaching with cheerful waves. The four of them exchanged warm greetings and soon found themselves deep in conversation. Ann mentioned, "Did you hear the crew safety drill this morning at 10? It was loud enough to wake my aunt from her nap!"

"Yes!" Jane chuckled. "It's the general emergency drill—just for crew training purposes, of course. They do it regularly, but it always causes a bit of a stir."

Samatha leaned forward. "I saw the announcements posted. No action required from us, thankfully. But what was suspended during the drill?"

Ann replied, "Quite a few things actually. All service stations close temporarily—no food or drink orders, and the shops on Decks 5 and 6 shut down. Even guest services had limited availability."

"That makes sense," Sean nodded. "Safety drills like these are essential. Keeps the crew sharp."

"And it was interesting to watch from the observation deck," Jane added. "Seeing the crew move in synchrony—it reminded me of how much goes on behind the scenes to keep us safe."

The conversation flowed naturally from there, turning into stories about previous travels, emergency procedures they'd witnessed on other voyages, and the impressive coordination of ship operations. Despite the grey skies outside, the warmth of new friendships and shared experiences created a glowing atmosphere inside the bar.

Later in the afternoon, as the drizzle continued tapping gently against the panoramic windows, Samatha suddenly put her hand to her stomach.

"Oh! Sean, have we even had lunch today?" she asked, wide-eyed.

Sean blinked. "Now that you mention it... no, we haven't."

They both burst into laughter. The main restaurants weren't open yet, and their stomachs rumbled in solidarity.

"Let's raid the Alfresco Pizza Grill," Samatha said mischievously. "I feel like having something naughty."

Minutes later, they found themselves at Deck 12, holding trays of beef burgers, chips, and cheesy pizza slices. Sitting at a casual table under the heat lamps, wrapped in warm jackets, they munched gleefully.

"This is probably the most fun we've had eating junk food in years," Sean said between bites, ketchup dotting his napkin.

Samatha giggled, taking a bite of burger and wiggling her feet. "We're like two schoolkids bunking class."

They clinked their fizzy drinks like champagne flutes and laughed again. Sometimes, it was the silly, spontaneous moments that created the fondest memories.

As they sat watching the drizzle bead along the glass panels of Deck 12, Sean leaned back in his chair, a thoughtful smile tugging at the corners of his lips.

"You know," he said, sipping the last of his cola, "at home, I've got a bit of a routine. Bit old-fashioned, I suppose."

"Oh, do tell," Samatha replied with a teasing grin. "I love a man with a breakfast plan."

Sean chuckled. "Every morning, first thing, I have a glass of water. Then I make breakfast, and I rotate it through the week—Monday is toast with marmalade, Tuesday is porridge with a dash of cinnamon, Wednesday I do scrambled eggs... and so on. Friday mornings are always a full English. But Friday nights—those are sacred."

Samatha raised an eyebrow with interest. "Oh? Sacred, you say?"

"Curry night," he said with a playful wink. "Every Friday, without fail. Usually a chicken tikka masala or lamb rogan josh. Bit of naan, poppadoms, and a good pint. It's a tradition going back decades in our house."

Samatha laughed, her eyes lighting up. "That sounds wonderful! You know what? You've just inspired me. Since tonight's still young, why don't we try the Indian restaurant onboard—Saffron, on Deck 12?"

Sean blinked. "You're serious?"

"Completely," she said, already rising from her chair. "Let's make it a Curry Friday at sea."

"I can't say no to that." He stood and offered his arm. "Lead the way, my Friday-night companion."

As the evening drew near, they returned to their cabins to get ready for their dinner at Saffron, the Indian restaurant on Deck 12. Wanting to embrace the spirit of the evening, they both chose smart-casual outfits with a touch of flair.

Sean wore a dark navy linen shirt tucked into slim grey trousers, complemented by polished leather loafers. He added a paisley-patterned pocket square in his jacket just for fun—a small detail that hinted at his excitement.

Samatha opted for a flowing crimson tunic with golden embroidery along the collar and cuffs, paired with tailored black trousers and low heels. She wrapped a soft pashmina shawl around her shoulders, its colors mirroring the deep hues of sunset. Her hair was loosely curled, and a hint of rose-scented perfume trailed her as she walked.

"You look radiant," Sean said as they met near the elevator.

"And you look quite dashing," Samatha replied with a warm smile.

Together, they stepped into the softly lit ambiance of Saffron, the aroma of spices already stirring their appetites and memories of Friday curry nights back home.

The atmosphere at Saffron was both intimate and vibrant. Low amber lighting bathed the room in a warm glow, while candlelit tables offered a sense of privacy amid the gentle hum of contented diners. Traditional Indian instrumental music floated softly through the air—sitar and tabla interlaced in calming rhythm. Ornate tapestries adorned the walls, and intricate lanterns hung from the ceiling, casting delicate shadows.

For starters, they chose crispy vegetable samosas and spicy lamb seekh kebabs, served with tangy tamarind and cooling mint chutneys. The combination of spices tingled on their tongues, sparking their appetites further.

For the main course, Sean opted for a hearty lamb rogan josh—tender chunks of meat in a rich, aromatic gravy. Samatha chose butter chicken, creamy and fragrant with just a touch of sweetness. They shared side dishes of saag paneer, garlic naan, fluffy basmati rice, and aloo gobi.

As Samatha took her first bite of the butter chicken, her eyes widened. "Oh my!" she gasped, quickly reaching for her mango lassi. "That's spicier than I expected!"

Sean burst out laughing, clearly enjoying the moment. "Didn't expect a firework in your mouth, did you?"

"I think my tongue just did a backflip," Samatha replied, fanning her mouth with her napkin. "Is this what you call flavor-packed?"

"Welcome to the spice club!" Sean grinned, offering her a spoonful of his milder saag paneer to cool things down. "Don't worry, it gets easier. Eventually."

They both laughed, and the moment became a shared joke, one they would no doubt tease each other about for the rest of the cruise.

For dessert, they indulged in warm gulab jamun—soft, syrup-soaked dumplings—and a shared plate of mango kulfi. To drink, Sean enjoyed a glass of red wine while Samatha chose a mango lassi that balanced sweet and creamy in perfect harmony, and helped cool her fiery palate.

As they savored each bite and exchanged stories over dinner, the restaurant's ambiance created a cocoon of comfort and connection. It was a meal to remember, made all the more special by the company they shared.

Later that evening, after returning to their cabins and slipping into more casual clothes, Sean and Samatha decided to cap off the night with a walk on the open deck. The rain had finally eased, and the clouds had parted just enough to reveal patches of starlight overhead.

They strolled quietly along the damp wooden planks, the sea stretching out in all directions like a silent, watchful guardian. The only sounds were the gentle hum of the ship's engines and the occasional creak of the railings as the vessel shifted through the waves.

Samatha leaned against the railing and looked up. "There's Orion," she whispered. "Just above the horizon."

Sean joined her, wrapping an arm around her shoulders. "It's moments like this that make it all feel timeless."

They stood there in silence, watching the stars appear one by one, each a tiny promise of light in the vast darkness.

"Do you think we'll ever come back to Norway?" she asked softly.

"I hope so," he replied. "But even if we don't, I'll always carry this moment with me."

Their fingers intertwined, they continued their walk under the emerging stars, hearts full and spirits steady, ready for whatever tomorrow's tide would bring.

After their stroll beneath the stars and a short break in their cabins, Sean and Samatha still felt energized. The hearty meal at Saffron had left them full, but the laughter and good conversation had stirred something more—a playful spirit they hadn't felt in a long time.

"Shall we test our trivia skills tonight?" Sean asked with a glint in his eye as they passed the ship's daily program posted near the lift.

Samatha leaned in. "You mean the *Friendly Feud* at the Purple Turtle Pub?"

"That's the one. I reckon we've collected enough random facts between the two of us to take on anyone," Sean said with a wink. "Besides, it's teams. We'll have each other's backs."

Samatha chuckled. "Well, I'm not promising I'll know anything beyond song lyrics and celebrity marriages—but let's do it!"

The Purple Turtle Pub was buzzing with energy. Dim lighting, vintage posters on the walls, and the comforting smell of hops created the perfect backdrop for an evening of good-humored competition. Passengers filled the booths and barstools, and the air buzzed with anticipation.

The host, a quick-witted cruise staff member named Theo, welcomed everyone with flair. "Tonight's showdown: *The Chums* versus *The Mates*! Who's got the answers? Who's got the laughs? And who's walking away with the bubbly?"

Sean and Samatha joined a team of equally enthusiastic guests calling themselves *The Chums*. Their opponents, *The Mates*, were already waving handmade signs and chanting.

The rules were simple: name the top five answers to a variety of questions surveyed from cruise guests. The faster and more accurately you guessed, the more points you earned.

First question: *Name something you always forget to pack for a cruise.*

Sean buzzed in with, "Toothbrush!"

Number two answer.

Samatha leaned into the mic. "Sunscreen!"

Number one.

Cheers erupted from *The Chums'* side.

Another round: *Name a famous British landmark.*

Sean and Samatha tag-teamed with "Big Ben," "Stonehenge," and "Tower of London." All on the board.

Samatha laughed so hard when one teammate confidently blurted "The Eiffel Tower," that tears welled in her eyes.

"It's a British landmark, love—not just a European one!" she called out amid giggles.

Question after question flew. From *Things you'd find in a ship's cabin* to *Excuses for being late*, the game kept everyone on their toes. Sean excelled at general knowledge and history, while Samatha shone in pop culture and food categories.

Their teamwork was seamless—teasing and celebrating, nudging each other with inside jokes. It felt less like a competition and more like a reunion of long-lost friends.

By the final question, *Name something people do on the last night of a cruise*, the room was nearly roaring. Samatha, with a sly grin, leaned forward.

"Panic pack their suitcase," she said, deadpan.

Theo howled with laughter. "Top answer!"

When the scores were tallied, *The Chums* were declared the victors. A bottle of champagne was presented, and cheers and applause filled the pub.

Sean held the bottle high. "To a night of fun, friendly feuding, and forgetting our troubles!"

"To friendship and fireworks!" Samatha added.

They left the Purple Turtle feeling triumphant and joyful, their minds light and hearts even lighter. The sound of their laughter lingered down the corridor, like echoes of youth reborn.

As they strolled arm in arm down the softly lit corridor, the laughter from the *Friendly Feud* still lingered in their voices. Sean gave a playful imitation of the cruise host's dramatic voice, and Samatha nearly doubled over laughing, clutching his arm for balance.

"Stop it!" she said between giggles. "I'm going to wake the whole corridor."

"But you know it's true," Sean grinned. "Your answer about panic-packing was gold."

They reached the door to Samatha's solo cabin. The hallway was quiet now, the hum of the ship a soft backdrop to their moment of calm. They stood there for a moment, smiles lingering, not ready to say goodnight.

"I haven't laughed like this in years," Samatha said softly.

"Me neither," Sean replied, his eyes kind. "It's like we've somehow stepped back in time tonight. Just a couple of kids, full of mischief and not a care in the world."

Samatha nodded, her voice just above a whisper. "I almost forgot how that felt."

They exchanged a long look—grateful, tender, understanding. A kind of silent pact passed between them: whatever this was, whatever it was becoming, it mattered.

"Goodnight, Sean."

"Goodnight, Samatha."

She slipped inside her cabin, the door closing with a quiet click.

Inside, she leaned back against it, smiling to herself. The room was dim and cozy. She moved to the bed, lay down, and stared up at the ceiling. Thoughts swirled—tonight's laughter, the rhythm of their connection, the way his eyes crinkled when he smiled.

It felt like youth again. Sweet, spontaneous youth—where the world was simple and joy came easily.

Across the hall, Sean was already drifting off in his own cabin, the covers pulled up to his chin. In his dreams, he was dancing barefoot at a school disco, hand in hand with someone who made him feel alive. The music was loud, the night endless, and he was young again—heart open, full of hope.

And somewhere in the gentle rocking of the ship, two solo travelers found a piece of their past rekindled—not just in memories, but in the warmth of shared company.

Two Solo Together

CHAPTER 12

Change of Course

At Sea, Norway – November 12, 2024

The Ship ship gently rocked through the open waters of the Norwegian Sea. Outside, a soft veil of rain tapped against the windows, and the wind stirred in playful gusts across the decks. The temperature hovered between 8 to 11°C—a classic northern chill, just crisp enough to encourage a lazy, indulgent morning.

Samatha awoke to the hush of the sea and the warmth of her cabin. The sky outside was a moody grey, casting a silvery glow through her window. She stretched under the covers and reached for the in-room phone.

"Room service, please. Yes, I'd like to order breakfast... for two."

A few minutes later, she knocked gently on Sean's cabin door, still in her robe and slippers, her hair loose from sleep.

"Sean? Fancy joining me for breakfast in my cabin? I've ordered too much."

Sean, already awake but still lounging in his own robe, chuckled. "You had me at breakfast."

Not long after, the familiar knock of room service brought a silver tray cart to her door. The steward wheeled it in with a polite smile, uncovering each dish with quiet ceremony.

Their breakfast was a feast for a slow sea day: warm buttery croissants, flaky pain au chocolat, and golden-brown pancakes stacked high with maple syrup and berries. There were also scrambled eggs with smoked salmon, grilled tomatoes, sautéed mushrooms, and crisp hash browns. On the side, a fruit platter sparkled with fresh melon, kiwi, and pineapple slices. Two glasses of freshly squeezed orange juice stood beside a steaming pot of English breakfast tea and a tall carafe of rich, dark coffee.

"Wow," Sean said as he sat by the window with his napkin tucked in. "You weren't kidding about ordering too much."

"I figured if we're going to be lazy, we might as well do it properly," Samatha said, settling into her chair and pouring them both a cup of tea.

Outside, the sea shimmered with rain and wind. Inside, the little cabin was a warm bubble of comfort—shared laughter, clinking cutlery, and the kind of breakfast that only ever tastes this good when there's absolutely nowhere else to be.

"I used to dream of mornings like this," Samatha said as she drizzled syrup over her pancakes. "No rush. No meetings. Just… peace."

Sean nodded, chewing thoughtfully. "It's strange, isn't it? We spend so much of life racing around, and now here we are, learning how to slow down again."

They lingered over their food, talking about nothing and everything. The rain continued to fall, the waves whispered against the hull, and for this little stretch of morning, the world outside faded away.

It was a sea day. And for once, neither of them needed anything more than a good breakfast, a window view, and the simple comfort of each other's company.

As they sipped the last of the coffee and nibbled the remaining bites of fruit, Sean leaned back in his chair with a mischievous glint in his eyes.

"You know," he began, dabbing his mouth with a napkin, "you really ought to enter the ship's photo competition."

Samatha raised an eyebrow. "Me? I'm not a serious photographer."

"Rubbish," Sean said with a grin. "You've been snapping brilliant photos every day. That one of the fjord mist rising behind the ship—pure magic. And don't even get me started on the shot of the reindeer at the Sami experience. That one deserves a gallery wall."

Samatha chuckled. "They're just holiday snaps. Nothing special."

"They're more than that," Sean insisted. "Look, I'll even pay the £3.99 entry fee. Consider it an investment. But if you win the prize, you have to split it with me."

She laughed, amused by the deal. "Is this your retirement business plan—backing photographers on cruise ships?"

"Only the talented ones," he replied, pouring them both another cup of tea. "And besides, you'll enjoy it. We can make a whole event out of it—choosing the right shot, printing it, submitting it. A bit of healthy fun."

Samatha tilted her head. "Alright then. But I get to choose the photo."

"Of course," Sean said, already reaching for his tablet. "Let's see what you've got."

They moved their plates aside and scrolled through Samatha's gallery of photos, leaning in together, laughing and reminiscing as each image brought back a memory. There was the selfie they took at the windy deck in Geirangerfjord, their rain-splashed smiles exaggerated by the gale. Then came the quiet elegance of Narvik Church, captured under a moody sky, and the wide-eyed curiosity of a polar fox from Sean's wildlife excursion—blurred but full of character.

"This one," Samatha said, pausing on a photo of the Saltstraumen whirlpools, the swirling water captured in a dramatic twist beneath an overcast sky. "This has something."

Sean whistled softly. "That's the one. Nature's power, beautifully framed."

They agreed on a few finalists, debating framing and titles, and giggling like schoolchildren over the silliest outtakes. The joy wasn't just in the competition—it was in the moment. In the shared creativity, the teasing, and the unexpected satisfaction of doing something just because it made them smile.

By the time they submitted the entry—titled *"Whispers of the Maelstrom"*—Samatha had forgotten all about the drizzle outside. The cabin was filled with light laughter and a growing sense of pride.

"Win or lose," she said, "this was worth it."

Sean clinked his teacup against hers. "Cheers to that. Now let's go win ourselves a bottle of bubbly."

After the fun of choosing the photo competition entry, Samatha stood up to clear away the breakfast tray, pausing to stretch her arms. "You know," she said, half to herself, "I think it's time I tackled my laundry. I'm starting to run low on fresh clothes."

Sean looked up from his tablet. "Ah, yes. The glamorous side of cruising," he said with a grin. "Ever thought about sending it off through the laundry service?"

Samatha nodded slowly. "I did look into that. There's something called *Magic Bag*—fill up one bag for £8, or two bags for £14.95. But honestly, the bags are quite small. You can barely fit in more than a few outfits. I think it's a bit pricey for what it is."

Sean chuckled. "I thought the same. My socks could bankrupt me on this cruise."

"I'd rather do it myself," she added. "But I wasn't sure where the guest laundry facilities are."

"You're in luck," Sean said. "There's a proper self-service laundry on Deck 10. Washing machines, dryers, even irons and ironing boards—all tucked neatly near the aft elevators."

Samatha looked relieved. "That's perfect! Is it usually busy?"

"Not too bad if you go during lunchtime or mid-afternoon. Most people are off the ship or at activities then. And don't forget to bring your own laundry pods—though they sell them in the shop if you've forgotten."

She smiled gratefully. "Thanks, Sean. That's a real help."

"No problem," he replied. "If you want, I can show you where it is later. Nothing says friendship like pointing someone toward a working tumble dryer."

They both laughed at the unexpected domesticity of cruise life—a little reminder that even in the middle of grand adventures and fine dining, everyday tasks still had their place. And somehow, even those felt a bit more fun when shared.

As Samatha folded the last of her laundry, Sean stepped out into the corridor to stretch his legs. He paused by the small silver letterbox affixed just outside their cabins and spotted a crisp envelope bearing their cabin numbers. Curious, he opened it and grinned.

"Samatha!" he called, waving the envelope. "We've got post!"

She emerged from her cabin, toweling her damp hands. "Post? On a cruise ship?"

Sean handed her the envelope. "Looks official."

She tore it open and read aloud: "You are cordially invited to join the *Solo Travellers' Lunch* at 12:00 PM today in the Buckingham Restaurant. This is a chance to reconnect with fellow solo guests for great conversation, shared stories, and a relaxed dining experience."

Her face lit up. "Oh, how lovely! I was hoping they'd organize something like this again. It's such a nice way to meet others who are on a similar journey."

Sean nodded in agreement. "Exactly. It'll be good to catch up with people we've seen at past solo events—maybe Anne and Jane will be there too."

They both felt a sudden twinge of excitement. The sea day had started slow and lazy, but now it had purpose. It wasn't just lunch—it was a chance to bond, laugh, and feel part of something more. As solo travellers, these little gatherings had become meaningful markers in their voyage—places where strangers turned into friends over soup and stories.

Samatha smiled. "Let's get ready, then. I think I'll wear that blue blouse I bought from the boutique yesterday."

"And I'll dust off my best solo-lunch shirt," Sean said with mock solemnity. "Time to impress the table with tales of whirlpools and spicy curry."

They shared a laugh, both secretly delighted to have something special to look forward to.

At exactly twelve o'clock, Sean and Samatha made their way down to the Buckingham Restaurant. As they entered, they were greeted by the soft hum of conversation and the welcoming clink of glasses. The grand dining room had been transformed for the occasion—white linen-covered tables were arranged in sociable clusters, each topped with fresh floral arrangements and elegant place settings.

A cheerful hostess greeted them at the door with a glass of champagne. "Welcome to the Solo Travellers' Lunch! Please, help yourselves—everything today is on the house."

Sean raised his eyebrows in delight. "Now that's a welcome."

As they moved deeper into the room, they were met with a surprising sight—solo guests filled the room from end to end, chatting animatedly and clinking glasses. A steward nearby confirmed the astonishing number.

"There are 123 solo travellers on this cruise," he said proudly. "Quite the community."

Sean looked at Samatha, eyes wide. "One hundred and twenty-three! I had no idea there were so many of us."

Samatha laughed, already sipping her mocktail. "It's like a secret club—suddenly revealed."

Tables buzzed with conversation. Waiters weaved between the guests offering trays of bubbling champagne, red and white wine, and colorful cocktails garnished with fruit. For those who preferred non-alcoholic options, there were mocktails of every kind—citrusy spritzes, creamy tropical blends, and refreshing berry mixes.

They took their seats at a round table near the window, joining guests from Canada, New Zealand, and Spain—each with their own story and reason for traveling solo. The menu was indulgent: delicate starters like prawn cocktail and goat cheese salad, hearty mains of roast lamb or grilled sea bass, and a dessert trolley filled with lemon tarts, eclairs, and rich chocolate mousse.

But it wasn't just the food or the drinks that made the lunch memorable. It was the atmosphere. Laughter rang out easily, strangers turned into friends over shared tales of previous ports and funny travel mishaps. Glasses clinked over toasts to freedom, to courage, to the joys of discovering the world one solo step at a time.

Sean leaned over to Samatha between courses, a smile tugging at his lips. "This has to be one of the best parts of the cruise so far."

She nodded, her eyes gleaming. "It's like finding your tribe, isn't it?"

"And did I mention," he added with a playful whisper, "the drinks are free?"

They both laughed, raising their glasses once again—grateful not only for the lunch but for the connection, the kindness, and the unexpected joy of being exactly where they were.

After the laughter and cheer of the Solo Lunch, Samatha and Sean took their time strolling through the ship. The rain outside had softened into a gentle mist, barely visible against the wide expanse of ocean, and the fresh breeze made the open decks feel brisk but refreshing.

They wandered through the art gallery on Deck 6, lingered in the library browsing books neither of them intended to finish, and eventually settled into the quiet comfort of the Observatory Lounge for a mid-afternoon cup of tea. Wrapped in the warmth of the ship and the companionship they shared, the hours at sea drifted by effortlessly.

Later that afternoon, the two of them made their way to the grand theatre, excited for the live performance of *The Last Tango in Berlin* — a highlight of the day's entertainment schedule. The Theatre @ Sea was already buzzing with anticipation. Plush red seats filled quickly, and the rich velvet curtains hung heavy with promise.

The lights dimmed, and the opening chords of dramatic music filled the space. The story transported them to June 1963, at the height of Cold War tension. President John F. Kennedy had just arrived in West Berlin, and beneath the surface of political pageantry, a shadowy mystery unfolded.

British spymaster George, dashing and dry-witted, was sent across the infamous Berlin Wall to investigate the murder of one of his top intelligence officers. What followed was a whirlwind of intrigue, double agents, miscommunications, and comic mishaps involving vodka, faulty disguises, a runaway tango competition, and an East German opera singer with a suspiciously perfect British accent.

Sean leaned in at one point and whispered, "It's like James Bond meets *Fawlty Towers*."

Samatha chuckled. "If Agatha Christie had written a comedy in a spy hat, this would be it."

The actors were brilliant — timing each punchline and plot twist with perfect flair. The audience roared with laughter when a scene involving an exploding briefcase and a chorus of mistaken identity unraveled into utter chaos.

By the end of the show, Samatha and Sean found themselves enthusiastically applauding with the rest of the audience. As the curtain fell and the lights came up, the two turned to each other with grins.

"So—who do you think did it?" Sean asked, eyes sparkling.

"I'm torn between the tango dancer with the glass eye and the KGB agent who was hiding in the wine cellar," Samatha replied, amused. "But I wouldn't be surprised if it turned out to be George's own secretary!"

Sean laughed. "My money's on the opera singer. No one sings *Ode to Joy* with that much flair unless they've got something to hide."

They bantered playfully about the twists and turns of the plot as they made their way out of the theatre, replaying their favorite lines and impersonating the overly dramatic spy characters.

It had been a perfect way to spend the afternoon—a bit of comedy, a touch of mystery, and just enough absurdity to lift their spirits and keep the laughter echoing long after the final curtain call.

As the ship cruised steadily through the North Sea, dusk began to settle across the horizon. The sky, a moody palette of grey and indigo, stretched out beyond the windows of their cabins, while inside, the gentle hum of the ship's engines was barely audible. Tonight was designated as a **smart attire** evening—a chance for guests to dress up, dine elegantly, and feel a little bit glamorous.

Sean stood in front of the mirror, adjusting the collar of his crisp white shirt. He wore a classic dark grey blazer, paired with tailored navy trousers and polished brown brogues. A subtle navy tie with a silver pattern completed the look. He smiled at his reflection, not quite used to dressing up these days, but appreciating the occasion all the same.

In her own cabin, Samatha took a little more time. She had chosen a sleek black evening dress, knee-length with delicate lace detailing at the sleeves and neckline. Around her neck was a simple silver pendant that had belonged to her mother, and she wore a pair of pearl earrings to match. Her makeup was soft and elegant, and she wrapped a light shawl around her shoulders for warmth.

When they met in the corridor just outside their cabins, Sean gave a small nod of admiration.

"You look absolutely stunning, Samatha."

Samatha smiled, a little shy. "And you look rather handsome yourself, Mr. Sean."

Arm in arm, they made their way down to **Deck 6**, where the **Buckingham Restaurant** was already abuzz with elegantly dressed guests. The atmosphere inside was refined but welcoming—crystal chandeliers sparkled overhead, white linens covered each table, and the soft clinking of cutlery blended with the mellow tones of a live piano playing in the corner.

Their waiter, a cheerful man named Paulo, led them to a window-side table set with glowing candles and a single red rose in a slender vase.

"Would you care for the wine list?" he asked with a warm smile.

"Yes, please," Sean said, accepting it with a nod. "A nice bottle of red to begin the evening."

For dinner, they indulged in a three-course meal that felt as special as the occasion itself. Samatha began with a smoked salmon roulade, delicate and rich, served with horseradish cream and pickled cucumber. Sean chose the wild mushroom risotto with truffle oil, savoring every spoonful.

For the main course, Sean ordered grilled duck breast with a cherry-port reduction, served with fondant potatoes and roasted root vegetables. Samatha opted for the pan-seared sea bass with lemon beurre blanc, accompanied by green beans and saffron rice.

They chatted easily between bites, discussing the play from earlier, their favorite parts of the cruise so far, and laughing again about the spicy surprise at Saffron the night before.

Dessert was a shared affair—Sean couldn't resist the sticky toffee pudding with vanilla bean ice cream, while Samatha ordered the dark chocolate mousse with a hint of orange zest. They traded spoonfuls and playful teasing, savoring every last bite.

As the meal wound down and the pianist played a soft rendition of "As Time Goes By," they both leaned back, content and relaxed.

"This," Samatha said, "feels like one of those perfect moments."

Sean nodded. "It does. Good food, good company, good memories. What more could we ask for?"

With full hearts and full stomachs, they rose from their table, thanked Paulo, and stepped back into the softly lit corridors of the ship, the elegant notes of the piano still echoing behind them.

As the elegant dinner progressed in the **Buckingham Restaurant**, the conversation at their shared table became lively and engaging. Sean and Samatha were seated with a group of fellow solo travellers—two women from Liverpool, a retired couple from New Zealand, and a gentleman from Edinburgh who had a sharp wit and a fondness for dry martinis.

Between the laughter and the exchange of travel tales, one of the women mentioned, "Have any of you heard about the **Navigational Chart Raffle**? They've got one up at the reception desk."

"The chart from the bridge?" Sean asked, intrigued.

"Yes, the very one," the gentleman chimed in. "A real nautical chart, signed by the Captain, Staff Captain, Chief Engineer, and the Hotel Director. It's a beautiful piece—framed and everything. Quite the collector's item."

Samatha leaned in with interest. "Oh really? I love things like that. How do you enter?"

"Tickets are £5 each," the woman explained. "Or three for £10. All the proceeds go to the **Crew Welfare Fund**. Helps support the crew with extra events, internet cards, even things like emergency support or recreation on board."

"I think that's a lovely idea," Samatha said thoughtfully. "I've seen how hard the crew works. Always smiling, always helpful."

Sean nodded. "And they've been so kind to us. I think we should both buy a few."

Samatha smiled. "Let's do three each. I'll pop by the reception desk on Deck 5 after dinner."

"And if you win," Sean added with a wink, "you'll have to frame it in your living room and invite me over just to gloat."

Samatha laughed. "Deal. But only if I don't have to pay you a finder's fee!"

Their tablemates chuckled, and the conversation moved on, but the thought of the raffle lingered warmly. It was another small thread in the tapestry of shipboard life—shared stories, good causes, and memories being charted one day at a time.

After their delightful dinner and engaging conversation at the Buckingham Restaurant, Sean and Samatha made their way to the **Palladium Lounge**, drawn by the promise of a soulful performance. The evening's entertainment featured **Emily Haig**, renowned for her soaring soprano vocals and emotive storytelling through song.

The lounge was bathed in soft, golden light, the stage framed with velvet curtains and subtle star-like spotlights twinkling above. Guests settled into plush seats with drinks in hand, the hum of anticipation settling into reverent quiet as the first notes of music filled the room.

Emily stepped onto the stage in an elegant sapphire gown, her presence both graceful and commanding. As she began to sing, her voice carried effortlessly through the space—clear, powerful, and hauntingly beautiful. Each piece she performed was introduced with a brief story, giving context to the lyrics and grounding the emotion in shared human experience.

She sang of love and loss, of home and journeys, of hope and remembrance. One moment she was tender and whisper-soft, the next she soared with operatic grandeur that sent shivers down the spine.

Samatha leaned in slightly, eyes glistening. "She sings like she's lived a thousand lives."

Sean nodded, visibly moved. "It's like her voice is painting memories in the air."

When Emily sang her final number—a heartfelt rendition of *Time to Say Goodbye*—there wasn't a dry eye in the room. The audience rose to their feet in a standing ovation, clapping and cheering with heartfelt appreciation.

As the crowd slowly filtered out, Sean and Samatha lingered in the warm afterglow of the performance, hearts quiet but full. They didn't need to speak much—the music had said everything that words could not.

They strolled back toward their solo cabins in companionable silence, their footsteps soft along the carpeted corridor, smiles still resting gently on their lips.

At Samatha's door, she turned to Sean. "Tonight felt... magical."

He nodded. "It did. Like the kind of night you want to bottle up and keep."

"Sweet dreams, Sean," she said softly.

"You too, Samatha. Youthful ones, if we're lucky."

They both chuckled quietly, then slipped into their cabins. And as the ship sailed gently through the northern waters under a curtain of mist and moonlight, their dreams were indeed sweet—full of music, laughter, and the warmth of newfound friendship.

Two Solo Together

CHAPTER 13

Change of Course

Bergen, Norway – November 13, 2024

The morning mist lingered as the ship quietly docked at **Bontelabo Pier** in **Bergen, Norway**, precisely at 8:00 AM. Raindrops tapped gently against the cabin windows, and the sea shimmered beneath a grey sky. With the temperature hovering between **6 to 11°C**, it was a damp but mild day, softened by a **gentle breeze** brushing in from the harbor.

Sunrise had just crept over the fjord-streaked horizon at **8:35 AM**, bathing the city's colorful wooden facades in a muted golden light, despite the clouds.

After freshening up, **Sean and Samatha** made their way to **Borough Market** for breakfast. The market buzzed softly with early risers and the familiar clatter of cutlery and cups. Under warm lighting and the comforting aroma of fresh pastries and brewed coffee, they found a cozy table by the window.

Sean ordered a plate of smoked salmon with scrambled eggs on sourdough toast, while Samatha indulged in a Norwegian-style breakfast: rye bread topped with cheese, cold cuts, sliced cucumber, and a soft-boiled egg. They shared a pot of strong coffee and a basket of warm cinnamon buns—soft, sticky, and dusted with sugar.

"It's hard to believe this is our last Norwegian port," Samatha murmured between sips of coffee.

Sean nodded, glancing out at the rain-speckled cobbled streets. "Let's make the most of it."

After breakfast, umbrellas in hand, they set off on foot toward Bergen's **city center**. The walk from the pier was scenic, lined with pastel-colored buildings, charming bakeries, and stores with displays of knitwear and glass art.

Their first stop was the **Bryggen Wharf**, a UNESCO World Heritage Site. The iconic rows of wooden Hanseatic houses stood tall and slightly crooked, their red, yellow, and white facades glowing against the grey sky. They wandered through the narrow alleyways between the buildings, peeking into artisan shops and photography galleries nestled within the timber structures.

Next, they visited **St. Mary's Church**, the oldest building in Bergen, dating back to the 12th century. Its heavy stone walls and austere beauty offered a peaceful moment of reflection, the faint scent of centuries-old incense still lingering in the air.

From there, they continued to the **Bergen Maritime Museum**, where Sean marveled at models of Viking ships and exhibits on Norway's proud seafaring legacy. Samatha was drawn to the historical maps and the stories of Arctic exploration.

As the rain eased into a fine drizzle, they made their way to the **KODE Art Museums**, where they admired works by Edvard Munch and other Nordic artists. The soft lighting and quiet halls created an atmosphere of calm as they moved from one gallery to another, occasionally stopping to share thoughts about a particularly striking painting or sculpture.

Time passed quickly in the cozy embrace of Bergen's culture and history. Around midday, they stopped at a small café near the **Fish Market**, where they warmed up with bowls of creamy fish soup, crusty bread, and more coffee.

By the time they headed back to the ship, the sun—now low in the sky—cast a silvery light on the rain-slick streets. Bergen's gentle melancholy had left a deep impression on both of them.

"Of all the places we've seen," Sean said as they approached the gangway, "this one feels like it belongs in a storybook."

Samatha smiled. "A rainy, beautiful chapter."

With one last glance at the misty harbor, they returned aboard, hearts full of quiet wonder, and ready to see what the rest of the journey would bring.

Before setting off deeper into Bergen, **Sean and Samatha** took shelter from the light drizzle in a familiar and inviting spot—**Starbucks**, just a short walk from the harbor. The scent of roasted beans and steamed milk wrapped around them as they stepped inside, a comforting contrast to the chilly breeze outside.

They ordered their favorites—**Sean** went for a classic **Americano**, while **Samatha** chose a **caramel macchiato**, treating herself to a little sweetness. They found a window seat, where they could sip their drinks and watch the flow of people on the wet cobblestones.

"Ahh, this hits the spot," Samatha said, blowing on her coffee and smiling.

Sean nodded. "No matter where we are in the world, there's always a Starbucks—and it's always warm inside."

As they slowly sipped, Samatha leaned forward with a gleam of curiosity in her eyes. "Do you fancy heading up to **Mount Fløyen**? The **funicular** goes straight from the city center. I've heard the view is stunning—even in this weather."

Sean took a thoughtful sip. "That does sound tempting. It's only a few minutes to the top, isn't it?"

"Yep. About six or seven minutes," she said. "There's a café and walking trails up there too. And if the clouds break just a little, we might get a magical view of the fjord and the city."

Sean tapped his cup. "What about **Mount Ulriken**? That one's higher, right?"

Samatha nodded. "Yes, it's the highest of the seven mountains. You take a **cable car** to the summit—it's more dramatic, I think. But it's a bit farther out from the city center, and we'd have to be mindful of the time."

Sean glanced out at the clock tower across the street. "True. We've only got until four o'clock before the ship departs. Maybe we do Fløyen today—save Ulriken for next time?"

"Agreed," Samatha said with a smile. "Besides, I don't know if I'm ready for more cable cars after the one in Tromsø!"

They both chuckled, recalling the swaying heights and gusty winds.

They finished their drinks, tossed their cups into the bin, and stepped back out into the light rain—refreshed, recharged, and ready to catch the **Fløibanen Funicular** up the mountain to chase a new perspective above the rooftops of Bergen.

As Sean and Samatha walked back from the harbor area toward the **Fløibanen Funicular station**, they heard familiar laughter echoing from the café terrace of a nearby hotel. Turning their heads, they saw **Ann** and **Jane**, waving enthusiastically from a corner table under a heated canopy.

"Well, speak of the fjord!" Sean said with a grin as he and Samatha approached.

Ann stood and pulled out a chair for Samatha. "You two just missed us—we've had *quite* the morning!"

"You look fresh from an adventure," Sean said as he sat down. "Where've you been?"

Jane sipped her tea and beamed. "We went on **two excursions** today—*Bergen & Fløyen Funicular* and *Bergen & Mount Ulriken Cable Car*. It was magical."

Ann nodded. "We started with the **Fløyen Funicular**. It leaves right from the city center—so convenient. The ride up only took about six minutes, but oh, the view! As we climbed, Bergen unfolded beneath us—the red-tiled roofs, the harbor, the narrow winding streets—all framed by misty hills."

"It was lightly raining," Jane added, "but the clouds floated just enough to give us that *Norwegian mystery*. When we reached the top, we could see across the fjords. There were trails everywhere, and goats, too—real mountain goats, just trotting around like they owned the place!"

"We had hot chocolate up there," Ann said. "And the little café was so cozy. If you get the chance, go. Rain or shine, it's worth it."

Samatha nodded eagerly. "That's actually where we're heading next. You've convinced me."

"But wait," Jane interrupted, "it gets better! After coming down, we hopped on a shuttle to **Mount Ulriken**. Now *that* is a proper mountain."

Ann leaned in. "You take the **Ulriksbanen cable car**, and I tell you—if you're not good with heights, hold on! It's much higher than Fløyen, and the ride takes about seven minutes. The wind started howling midway through, and the cable car rocked a bit— my heart was in my throat!"

Jane laughed. "She squealed, Sean. Like a child on a rollercoaster."

"I did not!" Ann laughed, swatting Jane's arm. "Well, maybe just a little. But the view from the top was *absolutely* worth it. Snow-dusted peaks, low-hanging clouds curling over the ridges—it was like looking out from the edge of the world."

"There's also a viewpoint platform," Jane said. "And they've got this glass floor you can stand on if you're feeling brave."

"No chance I was standing on that," Ann added quickly. "But it was lovely inside the mountain lodge café. We had cinnamon rolls and watched the clouds roll by. It was like being wrapped in a Norwegian fairy tale."

Sean raised his eyebrows, impressed. "You two really made the most of your day."

Ann winked. "That's the secret of cruising—maximize your hours in port!"

Samatha chuckled. "We might have to follow your lead."

The four of them chatted a little longer, exchanging tips on shops and hidden alleys worth exploring in Bergen. Then, as the skies brightened slightly, Sean checked his watch.

"Time for our own funicular ride," he said, rising. "You've officially inspired us."

"Enjoy every minute," Jane said, waving them off. "And don't forget to smile at the goats!"

Earlier that day, before the rain returned, Sean and Samatha had made their way to the top of **Mt. Fløyen** via the famous **Fløibanen Funicular**. The ride itself was a gentle climb, offering glimpses of wooden houses nestled into the hillside and forest trails weaving through pine trees. But it was the moment they stepped out onto the viewing platform that truly took their breath away.

Before them stretched the **city of Bergen**, cradled between mountains and fjords. The red, ochre, and cream-colored rooftops spilled down the hillside like a patchwork quilt, and the old Hanseatic buildings of Bryggen glowed softly in the morning light, despite the overcast sky. In the distance, the harbor shimmered with the quiet activity of ships and ferries coming and going, including their own cruise ship docked at **Bontelabo** pier — its white superstructure standing tall against the grey-blue sea.

"Would you look at that," Sean whispered, lifting his phone to take a panoramic shot. "We can see the entire harbor from here."

"It's like a painting," Samatha added, her eyes wide as she soaked in every detail — the layers of cloud hanging low over the fjord, the birds circling overhead, and the tiny splashes of color from boats moving through the channel. "It's hard to believe this is real."

After enjoying the views and walking some of the forested paths at the top, they made their way back down and later explored **Mt. Ulriken** by cable car. The journey upward offered a different perspective — steeper, more dramatic. As they ascended, the city seemed to shrink below them, giving way to sheer cliffs and the rugged beauty of Norway's mountainous terrain.

At the summit, the landscape changed completely. Windswept and raw, **Mt. Ulriken** revealed sweeping views of the **Seven Mountains** surrounding Bergen. From this higher vantage point, they could see well beyond the harbor — fjords snaking into the distance, small islands dotted with lone cottages, and the curvature of the coastline gently unfolding under the rolling mist.

Their cruise ship looked like a toy from up there — elegant, still, and dwarfed by nature's scale.

Samatha wrapped her scarf tighter as the breeze picked up. "Standing up here makes you feel… small, doesn't it?"

"In the best way," Sean replied. "It's humbling. You realise how much there is in the world to explore. How much beauty we often miss."

They stood in silence for a while, simply taking it in—the play of light on the water, the distant call of gulls, and the way the mountains seemed to guard the city below.

It was one of those moments where words became unnecessary—only the shared awe mattered. And long after they had descended, walked the streets, and made their way back onboard, the images from those viewpoints lingered in their minds like a postcard forever etched in memory.

By mid-afternoon, the light rain had returned, casting a silvery sheen over the cobbled streets of Bergen. The climb up **Mt. Fløyen**, the scenic views, and all the walking through the quaint city had finally caught up with them. Sean and Samatha, cheeks flushed from the cold and steps slowing with each block, began making their way back toward the port.

"I think my feet have staged a protest," Sean muttered, chuckling under his breath.

Samatha laughed, brushing a strand of damp hair from her face. "If they don't find me a seat and something sweet soon, there might be a mutiny."

Once they reached the gangway and stepped back onboard, they gave each other a look that said exactly the same thing: *We need tea and cake.*

Without hesitation, they made their way to **Dickens Lounge on Deck 5**, the cozy English-style tearoom with plush armchairs, polished wood paneling, and the comforting scent of fresh pastries wafting through the air.

As they walked in, the soft notes of a piano melody drifted from the corner, and the warmth of the room embraced them like a woolen blanket. They each ordered a hot drink—Sean went for a rich cappuccino, while Samatha chose a comforting chai latte. For their sweet reward, they picked slices of sticky toffee pudding and carrot cake, beautifully plated with cream and a drizzle of caramel sauce.

They sank into a sofa by the window, their coats hung over nearby chairs, and watched as the harbor slowly blurred behind droplets streaking the glass.

Samatha took her first bite of cake and let out a contented sigh. "This… is happiness."

Sean grinned, lifting his cappuccino. "To tired legs and sweet endings."

They clinked cups gently, and as the pianist shifted into a soft rendition of "As Time Goes By," the lounge filled with the quiet murmur of relaxed passengers and the occasional clink of china.

It was the perfect pause—no rush, no plans—just warmth, sweetness, and the shared comfort of knowing they'd made another memory worth savoring.

Back in their cabins after their afternoon treats at Dickens, Sean and Samatha took a little time to rest their feet and sip some water before getting ready for the evening ahead.

As they looked out from their windows, watching the harbor lights flicker in the early twilight of Bergen, the conversation naturally turned to dinner.

"The dress code tonight is formal," Samatha said, reading the daily programme leaflet left in their mail slot. "Dinner jacket or lounge suit for gentlemen... cocktail or evening dresses for ladies."

Sean chuckled. "Time to brush off the cobwebs from my bowtie, then."

"Oh yes," Samatha grinned. "And I brought that navy blue cocktail dress just for this kind of evening. I'd better try to remember how to walk in heels."

She laid out her dress on the bed—elegant and flowing with a touch of sparkle at the neckline—and began gathering her accessories: a silver clutch, pearl earrings, and a soft shawl to drape over her shoulders. In the mirror, she applied a subtle touch of makeup—enough to enhance the evening glow.

Sean emerged from his cabin in a classic black dinner jacket, crisp white shirt, and a neatly knotted black bowtie. He'd polished his shoes earlier, and his silver cufflinks caught the light just so.

"You look dashing," Samatha said with an approving nod as they met outside their cabins.

"And you," Sean replied, offering her his arm, "look like you've stepped out of an old Hollywood film."

They made their way toward the **Buckingham Restaurant**, and as they entered the grand corridor leading to the dining room, the atmosphere had already begun to shift. Passengers in gowns and tuxedos filled the halls, chatting in animated tones. There was a palpable buzz in the air—a mix of elegance, excitement, and good hum Near the entrance, they overheard a couple talking enthusiastically to another group.

"It's the big one tonight," a woman said, eyes shining. "They're doing the **Baked Alaska parade!**"

"Really?" her companion replied. "I haven't seen that in years. It's such a tradition."

Another passenger chimed in, "And the **parade of chefs**! All the kitchen staff come out—marching in a line, music playing, and each carrying those flaming Baked Alaskas. It's a tribute to their hard work."

Samatha leaned in toward Sean. "I love these old ship traditions. There's something so theatrical about them."

"I just hope the fire stays on the dessert and not the tablecloth," Sean whispered, making her laugh.

Inside the **Buckingham Restaurant**, the atmosphere was breathtaking. The chandeliers sparkled with hundreds of tiny lights, casting a golden glow across the white linen-draped tables. Silverware gleamed, wine glasses caught reflections, and the waitstaff moved like clockwork, weaving gracefully between tables with practiced precision.

Dinner began with an amuse-bouche followed by rich, sumptuous courses—lobster bisque, filet mignon, and pan-seared halibut among the evening's selections. Red and white wine flowed freely, laughter echoed through the room, and old jazz classics hummed softly from the live piano in the corner.

Then, as the main courses were cleared and the room dimmed slightly, a hush fell over the dining room.

A fanfare of music began.

The **parade of chefs** had begun.

From the double kitchen doors, a line of chefs emerged, dressed in pristine white uniforms and tall toques. Each held aloft a **Baked Alaska**—a dome of meringue covering layers of ice cream and cake, dramatically flambéed and glowing with small flames. Waiters followed with trays of more desserts, and the entire procession marched proudly through the restaurant to resounding applause.

The passengers rose to their feet, clapping and cheering, showing appreciation for the behind-the-scenes heroes of every meal.

Sean and Samatha joined in the applause with genuine smiles.

"That's the spirit of cruising, isn't it?" Sean said. "Celebrating food, people, and the joy of it all."

Samatha nodded, eyes glimmering in the candlelight. "It's magic. Like being part of a grand story."

As dessert was served—slices of Baked Alaska accompanied by berries and a drizzle of caramel—the conversation turned to the elegance of the night, the wonder of their journey, and the feeling that something truly special was happening, not just on the ship, but between them.

It was a dinner they wouldn't soon forget—a night of indulgence, celebration, and shared delight beneath the glittering chandeliers and gentle sway of the sea.

After finishing their exquisite Baked Alaska and lingering over a final glass of dessert wine, Sean and Samatha left the grandeur of the Buckingham Restaurant with full bellies and glowing smiles.

The ship's corridors shimmered with soft evening light as they strolled arm in arm toward the **Palladium Theatre**. The buzz from fellow passengers suggested tonight's performance—**"Dance Dance Dance"**—was not one to miss.

As they approached the entrance, Sean paused and turned to Samatha with a playful grin.

"You know what? Let's sit right at the front tonight—next to the oval part of the stage. I want to see every twirl, tap, and shimmy up close!"

Samatha laughed. "Front row? Bold move. You just want to be picked on by the dancers, don't you?"

"Maybe," Sean said with a wink. "But honestly, I just love a good show. And this one sounds like it'll be full of sparkle and energy."

They managed to find two perfect seats near the centre of the front row, just as Sean had hoped. The oval extension of the stage jutted out like a catwalk, giving them a nearly immersive view of the performance space.

The theatre filled quickly—laughter, chatter, and clinking glasses from the bar filled the air as everyone settled in.

The lights dimmed.

The curtain rose.

The first burst of music exploded through the speakers—lively, pulsing beats—and out came the dancers in a whirlwind of sequins, feathers, and flawless choreography.

"Dance Dance Dance" was a dazzling showcase of styles from around the world: samba, tango, jazz, tap, disco, even a cheeky bit of breakdancing. Each number brought with it a dramatic costume change, stunning lighting effects, and tightly synchronized moves that had the crowd cheering with every high kick and twirl.

Sean was enthralled.

His eyes followed every flick of a dancer's wrist, every pirouette and dip, and he leaned forward in his seat like a child watching fireworks.

"This is brilliant!" he whispered to Samatha halfway through, unable to contain his joy. "I feel like I'm at a Broadway finale!"

Samatha smiled, thoroughly entertained, although occasionally dodging a feathered costume or sequined swirl that came a bit too close to her seat. The energy from the stage was infectious.

Near the end of the performance, one of the dancers playfully blew a kiss to Sean as she spun past. Samatha burst out laughing.

"I knew you'd get attention sitting this close!"

Sean raised an eyebrow proudly. "I told you—front row is the only way to go."

As the final number reached its crescendo—a glittering, confetti-filled celebration of 70s disco—the audience erupted into thunderous applause. The standing ovation was instant, and Sean clapped until his hands stung.

"That," he said, turning to Samatha as the lights slowly rose, "was one of the best nights on this cruise so far."

"It really was," she agreed, still smiling. "I don't know if it was the show, the dinner, or your ridiculous face when the dancer flirted with you..."

"Probably a perfect combination of everything," Sean said with a grin.

Arm in arm, they exited the theatre with the rest of the glowing crowd, still humming the melodies of the final song. The ship gently swayed underfoot as they made their way back toward their cabins, the memories of the night swirling in their minds like the confetti that had rained from the ceiling.

Still buzzing from the energy of *Dance Dance Dance*, but ready to slow the rhythm of the evening, Sean turned to Samatha as they stepped out of the Palladium Theatre.

"Shall we end the night somewhere quieter?" he asked, his voice softer now, touched with contentment.

Samatha nodded. "I could do with something calm—maybe a drink and some gentle music?"

"Botanical Lounge, then?"

A few minutes later, they found themselves nestled into plush chairs in the cozy warmth of the **Botanical Lounge**. The space was transformed at night into a sanctuary of serenity—low golden lighting, gentle flickers of candles, and soft piano music drifting through the air. Potted ferns and blooming orchids created a tranquil oasis, with scents of lavender and jasmine lingering gently.

On stage, a classically trained pianist played a delicate rendition of *Clair de Lune*, each note floating like mist through the room. The music wrapped around them like a warm shawl, grounding their senses after the electric thrill of the earlier performance.

They sipped their drinks—Sean with a glass of cognac, Samatha with a herbal chamomile tea infused with honey—and spoke only in occasional whispers.

"I love that the ship offers both," Samatha said quietly. "The sparkle and laughter… and now, this."

Sean smiled. "It's the perfect ending. Letting the evening exhale."

As the pianist transitioned into a tender medley of familiar classics, the hush of the lounge seemed to slow time itself. The clink of glassware, the soft murmur of fellow guests, the ebb and flow of the sea outside the wide windows—it was all part of a peaceful symphony.

Eventually, they stood, stretching gently and exchanging a knowing glance—both tired, but content to the core.

"Solo cabins calling," Sean murmured with a yawn.

"Sweet dreams, Mr. Front Row," Samatha teased as they walked together down the quiet corridor, the ship gently rocking beneath their feet.

"Same to you, Miss Spice Queen," Sean grinned.

And with a soft laugh echoing behind them, they parted at their cabin doors. The night had been full of elegance, laughter, music, and joy—a blend of moments stitched perfectly together.

As they each drifted into sleep, the memories of Bergen, glittering stage lights, and soothing piano notes floated gently through their dreams—sweet, rich, and full of life.

CHAPTER 14

Change of Course

At Sea, Norway – November 14, 2024

The The last morning at sea greeted them gently. A fresh breeze stirred across the open decks, and soft clouds floated across a pale grey sky. The temperature had risen slightly—hovering between 10 to 13°C—but it was still cool enough to justify pulling on a cardigan or light jacket before stepping outside.

As Sean opened the door to collect the breakfast menu slip, he noticed a small printed note tucked inside their letterbox.

"Ah, here we are," he said, waving it as he returned inside. "Time change notice."

Samatha looked up from the vanity table where she was brushing her hair. "Oh, again?"

He unfolded the paper and read aloud: "Please note: the ship's clocks were set back one hour overnight. We are now returning to UK time."

Sean chuckled. "Funny thing, isn't it? I had to set my watch forward one hour when we arrived in Norway. Now, here we are—back on home time again."

Samatha grinned. "I guess time really does fly when you're having fun."

They both laughed, a bittersweet echo in the quiet of the room.

This final sea day was theirs to enjoy at a slower pace. With no port of call, the ship drifted steadily through the North Sea, a gentle lull marking the transition from one world back to another. There was something reflective in the air—an unspoken knowing that the end of the journey was near.

Sean made them each a hot cup of tea, and they stood by the window watching the low clouds roll across the horizon.

"We've done a lot, haven't we?" Samatha murmured.

Sean nodded, sipping. "And we've still got a full day ahead. Let's make the most of it—no regrets."

"Agreed," she said. "But first... breakfast. Shall we try somewhere new?"

Sean grinned. "Or we could go back to the Borough Market for one last round of eggs benedict?"

She smiled. "Perfect. One last breakfast ritual before we return to real life."

After taking a moment to enjoy the slow rhythm of the morning, Sean and Samatha decided to treat themselves to one final, proper breakfast at the **Buckingham Restaurant**.

"I think we deserve something a bit more elegant today," Sean said as they stepped into the lift.

Samatha smiled. "Agreed. No buffets, no trays. Just linen napkins, good coffee, and someone bringing us perfectly poached eggs."

The restaurant was already gently abuzz with early risers—solo travellers and couples chatting softly over silver teapots and fresh orange juice. Floor-to-ceiling windows offered a grey but calming view of the sea, while soft instrumental music played in the background, giving the space a dignified, serene energy.

They were shown to a window-side table set with polished cutlery and folded napkins. Their waiter greeted them with a warm smile and handed over the elegant breakfast menu.

Samatha took a deep breath and exhaled slowly. "This is lovely. It really feels like a farewell breakfast."

Sean nodded. "Let's make it count."

They ordered generously—Sean chose a full English breakfast with eggs sunny side up, crispy bacon, Cumberland sausage, grilled tomato, mushrooms, and a slice of fried bread. Samatha opted for smoked salmon and scrambled eggs on toasted sourdough, with a side of grilled asparagus.

To accompany it, they both had freshly brewed coffee, followed by warm croissants with butter and strawberry jam.

As they enjoyed the calm pace of the meal, they talked about their favourite parts of the cruise—Saltstraumen's whirlpools, the Indian dinner, the live shows, their laughter over spicy food, the quiet moments under the stars, and all the unexpected joys that had made the voyage special.

Sean smiled, looking around the restaurant. "It's amazing how quickly this place started to feel familiar. Like a second home."

Samatha nodded. "And it's not just the places we visited—it's the people, the little rituals. Even breakfast feels like a memory worth keeping."

They lingered over their coffee, neither in a rush to leave. Outside, the sea continued its gentle roll, carrying the ship—and all its stories—closer to home.

As they were finishing up the last of their breakfast coffee, a gentle *ding-dong* chime echoed across the ship, followed by a familiar voice over the ship's loudspeaker.

"Ladies and gentlemen, this is your Cruise Director speaking. A reminder for all guests who have purchased duty-free items: collection will begin this afternoon in the designated area near Guest Services. Guests in cabins on Decks 4 to 6 may collect their items at 2:00 PM. Guests on Decks 8 and 9 at 2:30 PM, and those on Decks 10 and 11 at 3:00 PM. Please bring your receipt and cruise card for collection. Thank you."

Samatha glanced over at Sean, arching an eyebrow. "Do you have anything to pick up? Any last-minute whiskey, or those giant Toblerones you can never say no to?"

Sean chuckled, dabbing his lips with his napkin. "Guilty. I picked up a bottle of single malt and a little perfume for my niece. Thought I'd treat myself since it's the last trip of the year."

Samatha grinned. "Very thoughtful of you. I bought nothing—just eyed up that jewellery for days and chickened out."

"There's still time," Sean said, nudging her playfully. "Or you could always pretend you forgot and blame it on the time change."

"I might just do that," she laughed. "Let's make a plan to collect your stuff at 3. I want to come and have a nosy at what everyone else splurged on."

"Deal," Sean nodded. "It'll be our last little mission on the ship."

With that, they stood and made their way out of the restaurant, strolling past others still lingering over breakfast, the gentle hum of chatter and clinking cutlery marking the slow, steady rhythm of this final sea day.

With the final sea day drifting by in a calm rhythm, Samatha looked out at the silvery waves through the glass corridor and sighed softly. "You know," she said, turning to Sean, "since it's our last day, I thought... why not take advantage of what we haven't done yet?"

Sean raised an eyebrow. "Such as?"

She smiled. "The hot tub. Deck 11. It's one of the few things I haven't ticked off my list. The swimming pool on Deck 12's been closed nearly the whole time because of the weather. But the hot tub's been bubbling away nicely—even in the rain."

Sean chuckled. "You want to go soak like lobsters on the last day?"

"Why not?" she grinned. "A little steam, some sea breeze, a chance to unwind before the dreaded packing begins. Come on—it'll be fun."

Sean shrugged in mock reluctance. "Oh fine. Twist my arm. I suppose if I must sit in warm water with a view of the ocean, so be it."

They returned to their cabins to grab swimsuits and towels, then made their way to Deck 11. The wind had eased slightly, and though clouds still swept across the sky, the rain had taken a break. The hot tub sat warm and inviting, steam rising lazily into the chilly air. A few other passengers were lounging quietly, letting the heat soothe away the weariness of travel.

Samatha dipped a toe in first, then sighed with delight as she sank into the bubbling warmth. "This… is heaven."

Sean followed, letting the hot water soak into his shoulders. "Not bad. Not bad at all."

They sat side by side, staring out at the endless ocean. It was peaceful up there—just the sound of water gurgling, seagulls in the distance, and the gentle thrum of the ship beneath them.

"I'm going to miss this," Samatha said softly. "The feeling of being suspended between sea and sky."

Sean nodded. "Me too. But at least we squeezed in one last little luxury."

They clinked their plastic cups of lemon water, pretending it was champagne, and shared a laugh.

For those few moments, the world slowed. No clocks, no packing lists, no goodbyes—just the warmth of the water, the salty air, and a friendship that had grown stronger with every mile sailed.

After their relaxing soak in the hot tub and a quick change into warm evening wear, Sean and Samatha made their way to the Theatre @ Sea for the early evening show. Tonight's performance was intriguingly titled *The Art of Murder*, a dark comedy set in the cutthroat world of the Parisian art scene.

The theatre buzzed with anticipation as the lights dimmed and the velvet curtains slowly drew apart. A spotlight hit the stage, revealing a lavish art gallery set—gilded frames, eccentric sculptures, and dramatic lighting casting long, moody shadows. A sleek, silk-suited narrator stepped into the light with a knowing smirk and opened the story with a flourish.

The plot unfolded around a flamboyant and egotistical gallery owner, a desperate artist with a dark secret, a rival critic with a thirst for scandal, and a wealthy patron who may or may not have a few bodies hidden behind her Monet collection. There were forged paintings, mistaken identities, mysterious poisonings, and at least one suspiciously overturned marble statue.

Samatha giggled through much of the performance, amused by the over-the-top dramatics and the cast's impeccable comic timing. But it was Sean who truly lost it—doubling over in laughter during a particularly absurd scene where the gallery owner dramatically faked his own death using a bottle of red wine, a feather boa, and a loudly misfiring fog machine.

"Oh no," Sean gasped, wiping tears from his eyes, "he's pretending to be murdered *in front of* the murder weapon!"

Samatha shook her head with a grin. "This is absolutely bonkers."

"But brilliant," Sean added. "It's like Agatha Christie got drunk in a Louvre gift shop."

The final act twisted wildly with every character accusing the others, all while still sipping champagne and posing for imaginary paparazzi. In the end, the mystery was solved—though how, neither Sean nor Samatha could quite explain. But it hardly mattered.

As the curtain fell and the cast took their bows, the theatre erupted in applause. Sean stood up clapping enthusiastically, still chuckling. "That was ridiculous and wonderful."

Samatha laughed. "Only on a cruise ship would you get a murder mystery wrapped in surrealist satire with a mime as a suspect."

"Best £0 I've spent on theatre," Sean said, still grinning from ear to ear.

Arm in arm, they left the theatre, their spirits lifted, still chuckling as they replayed their favorite scenes. It was the perfect kind of absurdity to end a perfect kind of day.

That evening, Samatha and Sean met outside the Buckingham Restaurant for their final dinner aboard the ship. The sky outside had grown dark, with only the faintest glow left on the horizon— just enough to silhouette the gentle waves rolling beneath them.

Samatha wore a deep plum-coloured blouse with a soft satin sheen, paired with black evening trousers and a delicate silver necklace. She carried a small white envelope in her handbag. "I got these from reception," she said, holding it up. "They're for the waiter and waitress. They've been looking after us for nearly two weeks, and they've been wonderful."

Sean nodded approvingly. "Good idea. It's nice to show some appreciation. They've made every meal feel special."

Inside the restaurant, the air was filled with quiet conversation and the gentle clink of silverware and glass. The service team moved graciously among the tables, dressed smartly in black waistcoats and crisp white shirts, smiling warmly at each guest.

Their usual waiter, a cheerful young man named Luis from the Philippines, greeted them with a grin. "Welcome to your last supper, Mr. Sean, Miss Samatha," he joked. "Tonight's menu is a special farewell."

They settled into their seats by the window and looked over the elegantly printed menu for the evening.

For starters, Samatha chose the *truffle mushroom arancini*—crispy risotto balls infused with earthy truffle and served on a bed of garlic aioli. Sean picked the *smoked salmon roulade*, delicately rolled with cream cheese and herbs, garnished with lemon zest and capers.

Then came the **soup course**—a rich *lobster bisque*, silky and fragrant, with a swirl of cream and a small puff pastry twist on the side. The warmth of it was soothing, like a hug in a bowl.

Next, they were offered a **fresh salad**: a classic *rocket and parmesan salad* with toasted pine nuts, cherry tomatoes, and a tangy balsamic glaze. Light, crisp, and a refreshing pause before the main.

For their **main courses**, Samatha chose the *grilled sea bass fillet* served on a bed of crushed new potatoes with asparagus spears and lemon butter sauce. The fish was perfectly cooked, with a crispy skin and tender, flaky flesh.

Sean, feeling nostalgic and a bit indulgent, opted for the *slow-cooked beef short rib* with red wine jus, creamed parsnips, and honey-glazed carrots. The meat fell apart with the touch of a fork, rich and comforting.

As they sipped their wine—Sean with a bold Merlot, Samatha with a crisp Pinot Grigio—they shared their thoughts on the journey.

"I'm going to miss this," Samatha said, taking a slow bite of her sea bass. "The food, the quiet elegance, the routine of dinner at the same table with you."

Sean smiled. "Well, we'll just have to recreate it back home. You can bring the envelope; I'll bring the beef."

For dessert, they both chose the signature *bakewell tart with clotted cream*—a tribute to classic British comfort. It arrived warm, its buttery pastry and almond filling melting together perfectly. On the side, a quenelle of clotted cream and a streak of raspberry coulis added the finishing touch.

With their coffee, a surprise arrived: a small plate of **petits fours**— bite-sized truffles, macarons, and chocolate-dipped strawberries.

Before leaving, Samatha discreetly placed her white envelope on the edge of the table. Luis spotted it and gave her a knowing nod, his smile soft with gratitude.

Outside the restaurant, the evening air was cooler now, but still pleasant. The ocean stretched out endlessly in the moonlight as the ship sailed smoothly into the final night.

"Well," Sean said as they paused in the corridor, "that was one fine farewell feast."

Samatha linked her arm with his. "Perfect ending to a perfect voyage."

They walked off together, ready for their last evening at sea.

After dinner, with warm bellies and even warmer hearts, Samatha and Sean made their way to the Palladium Theatre for the final live show of the cruise: **"Modelled by Soul & Motown."** The theatre was already buzzing with excitement as guests found their seats, chattering with anticipation. The stage glowed with rich, golden light, and a live band tuned up in the pit.

From the moment the curtain rose, the room came alive.

The show exploded into high energy with a rousing medley from *The Four Tops*, followed by back-to-back hits from *Stevie Wonder* and *The Jackson 5*. Soulful vocals soared, tight harmonies filled the air, and the stage lit up with polished choreography and vibrant costumes that shimmered under the spotlight.

Sean tapped his foot in time, grinning from ear to ear. "This is my kind of party!" he said over the music.

By the time the performers launched into *"I Want You Back"* and *"Ain't No Mountain High Enough"*, the entire room was moving. Guests clapped, sang along, and many began dancing in the aisles.

Sean turned to Samatha with a spark in his eyes. "May I have this dance?"

Laughing, she placed her hand in his. "You better keep up!"

They danced together in the aisle, swaying and spinning under the theatre lights, surrounded by fellow cruisers who had all shed their inhibitions for one final celebration at sea. It felt spontaneous, joyful—like the cruise itself had taken on one last breath before the journey's end.

As the final number ended in a flourish of lights and confetti, the performers exited the stage only to return moments later—this time walking through the aisles. One by one, dancers, singers, and musicians lined up in a grand farewell procession stretching from the stage to the back of the theatre. Each one offered waves, hugs, and handshakes to the audience.

Many guests stood to applaud, take photos, and say their goodbyes. Some wiped tears from their eyes. Others simply beamed, holding their phones high to capture the moment.

Samatha held up her camera, snapping a few shots as a keepsake. "This… this is the kind of ending you never forget," she said softly.

Sean nodded, eyes a little misty. "They really know how to say goodbye."

Hand in hand, they slowly walked out of the theatre with the crowd, surrounded by smiles, laughter, and the echo of Motown classics still ringing joyfully in their ears.

Later that evening, after the show and after the final photos were taken, Sean and Samatha found themselves lingering on the open deck, the breeze gentler now, carrying the salty scent of the sea and the faint echo of music from inside.

They leaned against the rail in silence for a while, the stars blinking faintly above, the ship gliding smoothly through dark waters. The horizon was a quiet line between sea and sky, but the weight of the moment settled softly between them.

"I can't believe it's almost over," Samatha said, her voice barely above a whisper.

Sean turned to look at her, his expression thoughtful. "Two weeks. Just two weeks. Feels like I've known you far longer."

She gave a small laugh, then shook her head. "I came aboard expecting to be alone. A little quiet, maybe some walks and books… but then—" she smiled at him, "—then there was you."

He smiled back, but there was something in his eyes—a tenderness, a quiet ache. "It's strange, isn't it? How quickly you can connect with someone. Day after day, moment by moment, suddenly they become part of your rhythm."

"We've had so many laughs," she said, thinking back to curry night, dance nights, lost gloves, shared pizza, the boat rides, the jokes that made no sense to anyone else.

"And so many good talks," Sean added. "I think I learned more about myself from talking to you than I have in years."

A silence stretched between them again—peaceful, full of unsaid words.

Samatha looked out at the sea. "Do you think this is it? Just a holiday friendship?"

Sean hesitated, then shook his head. "No… I think it's more than that. Whatever comes next, I'll carry this with me. Us. These memories."

She nodded, eyes glistening. "Me too."

They stood there a little longer, the air cool against their skin, the moment warm in their hearts. Whatever waited for them beyond this ship, one thing was clear—they had changed each other's journey. A bond had been formed, not by time, but by presence, laughter, honesty… and something gently unspoken.

After the theatre show and a stroll along the quieter corridors, Sean and Samatha decided it was time to call it a night. They returned to their solo cabins, where the bittersweet reality of the last evening at sea settled in.

The usual cheerful chatter between them faded into a calm and reflective silence as they unzipped their suitcases and began to pack. The room felt different now—less like a temporary adventure hub and more like a space they were reluctantly preparing to leave.

Samatha carefully folded her clothes, trying to keep her souvenirs safe between layers of sweaters and scarves. She paused to look at a postcard she had picked up in Bergen—a painted view of the harbor from the mountaintop. "Hard to believe it's almost over," she murmured to herself.

In the hallway, Sean knocked lightly on her door. "All packed in there?" he asked, peeking in with a sheepish grin.

"Almost," she said, gesturing to her half-filled suitcase. "Still deciding how to wedge in this awkwardly shaped candle from the Christmas market."

Sean laughed. "You know, I've had to sit on my suitcase twice now. It's the universal sign of denial."

As they both zipped the final compartments, Sean looked down the hallway at the line of suitcases already appearing outside doors. "We've got to put ours out before midnight, right?"

Samatha nodded. "Yes. The tags are already on mine. I'm just giving it a goodbye pat."

As Sean lifted his bag upright, he turned to her and asked, "Hey, by the way… did you ever cash out those chips you won at the casino the other night?"

Samatha blinked, then gasped. "Oh no! I completely forgot!"

He raised his eyebrows. "Samatha! You won, what—£30 in chips?"

"£35 actually," she said proudly. "That's a decent bottle of gin!"

"Well, you'd better run down there and get it, unless you want to leave the ship a mysterious high roller," Sean teased.

She rolled her eyes but grinned. "I'll do it first thing in the morning. Or maybe I'll keep them as a souvenir of my one moment of gambling glory."

"You'll have to frame them like a trophy," Sean said. "Right next to your certificate of bravery for trying spicy food."

They both laughed, and then the hallway grew quiet again as more doors closed and the soft hum of suitcase wheels echoed in the background.

"Sleep well, Samatha," Sean said warmly. "See you for breakfast?"

"Wouldn't miss it," she replied. "Goodnight, Sean."

They disappeared into their cabins, hearts full, bags packed, and minds already drifting between memory and dream—savoring one last night of the sea's gentle rocking.

When they finally turned to go back to their cabins for the night, it wasn't with sadness—but with gratitude. For the friendship that had bloomed unexpectedly, and the comfort of knowing that some connections, once made, never really go away.

CHAPTER 15

Change of Course

London Tilbury – November 15, 2024

The ship arrived back at **London Tilbury** just as the first rays of morning sun broke across the Thames. It was a clear, crisp day—**4 to 11°C**, with golden sunlight glinting off the river and a gentle breeze rustling the Union Jack at the stern. After days of misty fjords and Norwegian drizzle, the return to English sunlight felt oddly poetic.

Sean's alarm buzzed gently at **6:15 AM**, pulling him from a restless sleep. It was disembarkation day, and the ship was already slowly gliding toward **Tilbury**, its journey nearly complete.

Across the corridor, Samatha was already awake, sipping tea by the window in her solo cabin. The view outside showed the early morning light just beginning to touch the horizon, casting a pale gold across the waters of the Thames. A tugboat chugged alongside them, and the London skyline loomed softly in the distance.

They had both packed the night before, placing their suitcases outside their doors as instructed. But the final morning still felt rushed and surreal.

A notice slipped under the cabin door the night before had read in bold letters:

"**IMPORTANT** – All guests must vacate their cabins by **7:30 AM**. Please bring your hand luggage and all valuables with you. Breakfast is available in designated venues."

Sean knocked gently on Samatha's door at 7:00 sharp, both of them already dressed, bags slung over their shoulders.

"Morning," he said with a tired smile.

"Morning," she echoed, her voice soft but steady. "Feels strange, doesn't it?"

They walked together down to the **Buckingham Restaurant**, which was already buzzing with guests having their final onboard meal. The crew, though smiling and gracious as ever, moved with the efficient rhythm of turn-around day.

Their table was set simply—white linen, polished cutlery, a sense of closing ceremony. They ordered a light breakfast: scrambled eggs, toast, grilled tomato, and a pot of tea. They didn't speak much—there was something bittersweet in the air, a mix of satisfaction and reluctance.

Just after 7:00 AM, a calm voice came over the ship's public address system:

"Good morning, ladies and gentlemen. This is your Cruise Director speaking. Welcome back to Tilbury. Disembarkation will begin shortly, starting with Deck 4 forward. Please listen carefully for your deck and colour group to be called. Guests are reminded to have their cruise cards and passports ready. Thank you once again for sailing with us—on behalf of the captain, officers, crew, and entertainment team, we wish you a safe journey home."

The familiar chime of the speaker faded, leaving a quiet hum of activity around the ship as passengers moved slowly, many with mixed emotions, toward their final hours on board.

At **7:28**, they stood outside their now-empty cabins one last time, checking and double-checking for forgotten chargers or souvenirs left behind.

Sean looked down the corridor. "We've officially been evicted."

Samatha chuckled. "Just as I was starting to feel at home."

They rolled their carry-ons toward **Deck 5**, joining other guests in the waiting lounge by reception, where final announcements and colour-coded groups were called. Outside the windows, the terminal came into clear view, and crew began preparing the gangway.

Sean leaned close. "What do you say we grab one last coffee before we leave the ship forever?"

"Only if we toast to everything that's happened," Samatha replied.

"Deal."

After breakfast and final cabin checks, Sean and Samatha made their way to **Borough Market Café** on Deck 6 for a last cup of coffee. The ship had just docked at **London Tilbury**, and the first rays of the morning sun were pouring in through the tall glass windows, warming the café in golden light.

As they approached the counter, they spotted familiar faces—**Ann and Jane** were seated at a corner table, chatting animatedly over cappuccinos and croissants.

"Morning, strangers!" Jane called with a bright smile. "Come join us—we saved you two seats!"

Sean and Samatha gratefully slipped into the booth. The conversation quickly turned to the disembarkation process now underway.

As they sat with Ann and Jane in the warm corner of Borough Market Café, the ship's overhead announcement chimed gently through the speakers.

"Ladies and gentlemen, good morning. This is your Cruise Director speaking. UK Customs and Immigration have now cleared the ship. Disembarkation will commence shortly, beginning with Priority guests. Please proceed to your designated lounges as indicated on your disembarkation letter. We kindly remind all guests that cabins must be vacated by 7:30 AM, and all guests must disembark by 11:00 AM. Thank you for cruising with us."

Sean leaned back slightly and nodded thoughtfully. "Right on time. Disembarkation starts at **8:45 AM**, and by **11 o'clock**, this ship will be completely emptied out. It's hard to believe, isn't it? How quickly it all turns over."

Samatha sipped her tea. "It feels strange… Like everything is shifting into a new rhythm."

Jane pulled out the folded **disembarkation leaflet** from her bag and tapped it. "It's all very well organized this morning. Did you see the schedule?"

Ann nodded. "Our friends in the **Priority Suites** have to wait in **Aces & Eights**—they're in the first group to disembark."

Jane added, "We're on **Deck 10**, so we're assigned to the **Observatory Lounge**. People from **Deck 11** are gathering in the **Botanical Lounge**, and the ones on **Decks 4, 5, and 8** go to the **Palladium Show Lounge**."

"Oh, and **Deck 6** waits in the **Purple Turtle Pub**," Ann said, sipping her coffee. "Each group has a colour-coded tag to match their luggage. When they call your colour, it's time to head out."

Sean gestured toward the window, where port staff could be seen organizing luggage carts and placing colour-coded tags in neat rows. "You know, by **1 PM**, the new guests for the next voyage will begin arriving. Fresh faces, new stories, the same ship but a different adventure. It's like the clock resets."

Jane smiled wistfully. "A floating city, always in motion."

Ann added, "And we were part of it—if only for two weeks. Now it's someone else's turn."

Samatha raised her brows in admiration. "That's actually really impressive. With over a thousand passengers, it could've been chaos—but this is smooth. The way they've broken it down by deck and lounge makes everything flow without crowding."

Sean glanced out the window toward the terminal, where disembarkation officers were already in place. "It's like a military operation—only with better breakfast."

They all laughed, the tension of departure eased just a little by friendly company and warm coffee.

Jane smiled, looking around. "You know, we've been on quite a few cruises, and I have to say—this one really stood out. Not just for the ports and shows, but for how well they handle the little things. Even saying goodbye."

Ann added softly, "It helps that we met such wonderful people along the way."

Samatha and Sean exchanged a glance and a nod, their hearts full from the shared journey.

The four of them sat for a few moments in quiet reflection, watching the terminal bustle with activity. Stewards moved efficiently through corridors, tidying up cabins, changing linens, and resetting dining rooms. The atmosphere aboard had subtly changed—still warm, but now humming with the pulse of transition.

Sean turned to Samatha and smiled. "Makes you think... maybe one day we'll be back too. On a different cruise, different route— but still this same feeling of wonder."

She nodded. "Yes. And next time, maybe we'll be the ones welcoming first-timers aboard."

They all laughed gently at the idea, a comforting thought in the midst of farewells. The journey was ending, but the sea—like memory—never truly stands still.

As they sat side by side in the Observatory Lounge, sipping their final coffees and waiting for their disembarkation group to be called, Samatha unfolded the **Daily All Aboard** newsletter from the small table beside her. She scanned the last page, her eyes widening slightly.

"Sean," she said with a tone of amazement, "did you know we've travelled **3,470 nautical miles** over the last 14 days?"

Sean raised an eyebrow, leaning in to glance at the paper. "That's quite a journey. Feels like it too—though I could happily go another 3,000 miles."

Samatha smiled, continuing, "We visited **nine ports**. I can't believe how much we've seen in just two weeks."

"From the fjords of Norway to every onboard show you could squeeze in," Sean grinned. "I'd say we made the most of every mile."

She nodded. "And look here," she pointed at a small chart at the bottom of the page. "They've listed the number of **crew members** and their nationalities. It says there are **563 crew** from **30 different countries**."

Sean leaned closer, intrigued. "Now that's impressive."

Samatha began reading aloud:

"227 from India, 164 from Indonesia, 94 from the Philippines…"

Sean interrupted, "That explains why every time I pass the kitchen, I smell the best curry."

Samatha laughed and continued, "**22 from the United Kingdom, 8 from Ukraine, 8 from Myanmar**…"
She paused and looked up, "This is such a diverse team. No wonder the service is so seamless. Everyone brings something unique."

Sean nodded thoughtfully. "You know, it takes more than just good training—it takes a real team effort. And living on board for months at a time, they become like family."

Samatha continued, scanning the list:

"**4 from Brazil, 4 from Mauritius, 3 from Romania, 3 from Sri Lanka, 3 from Venezuela**… then **2 each from Bhutan, Bulgaria, Greece, Hungary, Russia, Serbia**..."
She paused again. "And listen to this—**one crew member each from Colombia, Ghana, Kenya, Moldova, Montenegro, Norway, Peru, Spain, Tunisia, Turkey, and Zimbabwe.**"

Sean whistled softly. "One big floating United Nations."

"Exactly," Samatha said with admiration. "And yet, everything ran like clockwork. From housekeeping to entertainment, the restaurants to reception… I can't imagine the coordination behind it all."

"They've done a brilliant job," Sean agreed. "You know, sometimes we take it for granted—fresh towels, perfect meals, smiling faces, even when the sea's rough. These folks work so hard behind the scenes."

Samatha gave a small, respectful nod. "It makes you want to say a proper thank you, doesn't it?"

"I did," Sean said. "Left something extra in that little white envelope."

Samatha smiled knowingly. "So did I."

They both fell quiet for a moment, watching as passengers moved past the panoramic windows, waving goodbye to crew members, taking their final selfies on the ship.

"I'll miss this," Samatha said softly.

"Me too," Sean replied. "But hey, who says it has to be the last one?"

They exchanged a smile, the kind of smile that only comes from shared memories and a promise to not let them fade.

Sean and Samatha stood by the railing on Deck 10, watching the port come into view. Lorries moved in the distance, and terminal staff in neon vests bustled about preparing for the day's flow of passengers. Tugs and ferries moved across the river, and overhead, gulls wheeled lazily in the sky.

"So… this is it," Sean said, his voice soft.

Samatha nodded, hands resting on the metal rail. "Back to real life."

They both wore warm jackets over their travel clothes, their luggage already placed outside their cabins hours before. In each of their eyes was a trace of longing—for the rhythm of ship life, the charm of discovery, the unexpected joy of companionship.

As they slowly made their way back to the corridor near the gangway, Samatha noticed a cluster of large suitcases neatly lined up against the wall. Each had a brightly coloured label that read "**Victoria Coach**" in bold, easy-to-spot letters.

She paused, puzzled. "Sean, look at those labels. They say *Victoria Coach*, not Tilbury or anything about the ship. What's that about? Are those guests taking a different route?"

Sean glanced over and smiled knowingly. "Ah, yes—those are for guests using the cruise line's **Victoria Coach Station luggage transfer service**."

Samatha tilted her head. "So... the cruise sends their suitcases directly to London?"

"Exactly," Sean said, adjusting his shoulder bag. "It's quite clever, actually. For those who've pre-booked, the cruise company arranges for their luggage to be taken straight from the ship and delivered securely to *Victoria Coach Station* in central London. That way, guests who are taking the coach—or even those connecting by train or tube—don't have to lug their bags around. They just pick them up at the station when they arrive."

Samatha nodded slowly, impressed. "That's... surprisingly convenient."

"Oh, and it's not just for coaches," Sean added. "Some guests took advantage of other **transfer services** too. There are trains directly to Tilbury, and the company offers **optional rail or coach packages** when you book the cruise. Sometimes they even throw in **free transfers** as part of a special promotion."

"Really?" Samatha raised an eyebrow. "Like free transport from London to the ship?"

"Yep," Sean confirmed. "Or free **car parking** at the port if you prefer to drive yourself. Depends on the deal at the time. I remember reading some people from the North even got **connecting coaches from other cities**. It's all organised by the cruise line so everyone arrives smoothly."

Samatha looked thoughtfully toward the baggage line. "That explains why I saw such a mix of people on board—some came by car, others by train, and now some leave with just a small hand-luggage bag. Meanwhile, their suitcases go off on their own journey."

Sean chuckled. "It's a whole **logistical orchestra**, this cruise business. They've done it so many times, it's practically a science."

"It's impressive," she said. "I wouldn't mind trying that service next time. Makes everything easier, especially for solo travellers like us."

"Exactly," Sean agreed. "And it's just one more way they make people feel looked after—even right to the end of the trip."

They both watched as a staff member wheeled another batch of *Victoria Coach*-tagged suitcases toward the waiting transport van, efficiently and almost silently. The journey was ending, but the attention to detail hadn't skipped a beat.

As they stood near the gangway area, watching the final waves of guests being guided to their designated lounges, a familiar *ding-dong* echoed through the corridor, followed by the calm voice from the ship's speaker system:

"Miss Samatha Collins, please come to Reception on Deck 5 at your earliest convenience. Miss Samatha Collins to Reception, Deck 5. Thank you."

Samatha froze mid-step and blinked. "Oh... that's me."

Sean turned to her with a curious look. "Did you forget to check your onboard account?"

She gave him a sheepish glance. "Possibly. I was going to double-check everything after dinner last night, but then we got caught up in the show, and—well—you know how it went."

He nodded. "You think it's about the final bill?"

"Maybe," she said with a frown. "Or it could be something with my card. I had a text from the bank the other day, asking to verify a charge. I thought I sorted it, but..." Her voice trailed off as she reached into her bag for her cruise card and wallet. "Best I go down and set it straight now. I don't want any hold-ups later."

"I'll come with you," Sean offered immediately. "No point in waiting here on my own."

She smiled gratefully. "Thanks. Hopefully, it's nothing major."

They made their way to the lifts and headed down to Deck 5, weaving through the last bits of morning bustle. At Reception, a line of guests stood checking out, asking questions, and sorting luggage matters, but the staff moved quickly and efficiently.

"Miss Collins?" a staff member in a navy-blue uniform greeted her with a kind smile. "If you could step over here, please."

Samatha followed, while Sean stayed a few paces behind, watching quietly. The receptionist tapped a few keys, then looked up gently.

"It seems your credit card didn't go through for the final transaction overnight. It might just be a verification issue. Do you have another card, or would you like to try the same one again?"

Samatha pulled out the same card and offered a friendly but apologetic smile. "I'll try this one again. If not, I've got a backup."

A few quick steps at the card reader, and this time, the transaction went through without issue.

"Done!" said the receptionist cheerfully. "All settled now. Thank you, Miss Collins. You're all cleared for disembarkation."

Samatha sighed in relief. "That's a weight off. Thank you so much."

She turned to Sean with a grin. "All sorted. Crisis averted."

He smirked. "Good. You were almost about to be the last person dragged off the ship by security."

They both laughed and walked together back toward the main lounge area, where the final announcements for disembarkation were beginning to sound again.

Their cruise was nearly over—but the companionship, laughter, and easy camaraderie between them still felt very much alive.

As they left the reception area and rejoined the flow of passengers in the main corridor, Sean glanced at the growing line forming toward the gangway. He leaned a little closer to Samatha and said, "You know, some of my friends opted for express disembarkation."

"Express disembarkation?" she echoed, curious. "What's that?"

"It's a service for guests who need to get off the ship early— usually because of early flights or tight connections," Sean explained. "But the catch is, they have to carry all their luggage off themselves. No porters. No leaving it outside the cabin the night before."

Samatha raised her eyebrows. "That sounds like a bit of a hassle."

"Exactly," Sean nodded. "One of my mates—Tom—he and his wife are flying out from Heathrow to New York this morning. Their flight's at 11:30. So they wanted to be among the first off the ship."

"Oh wow. That's cutting it close," she said, glancing at her watch. "Heathrow's at least an hour and a half from here, isn't it?"

"Yeah, even longer with traffic," Sean said. "But they booked a private transfer and requested express disembarkation when they checked in at the beginning of the cruise. Their bags were already by the door at 6 a.m. this morning."

Samatha shook her head with admiration. "I suppose it makes sense if you have tight plans. Still, I don't think I'd want to be dragging two weeks' worth of clothes and souvenirs off the ship at dawn."

Sean laughed. "Nor me. Especially after all that shopping we did in Bergen and Flam. I'd probably pull a muscle."

They both chuckled, then stepped aside to let a porter through, wheeling a trolley piled high with luggage.

"You've got to admire the logistics though," Samatha added, glancing at the hustle around them. "This cruise line really knows how to handle it all—normal disembarkation, express services, Victoria Coach luggage deliveries. It's like a military operation."

Sean grinned. "Well-oiled machine. I'd hate to be the guy coordinating it all, but they make it look easy."

As the announcements continued, they looked over the last crowds of passengers sipping their final coffees, checking cabin keys one last time, and saying goodbye to staff members with hugs and photos. The atmosphere was bittersweet—an end to something memorable.

After nearly an hour of waiting in their designated lounge, the announcement finally came through the ship's PA system:

"Ladies and gentlemen, may we now invite guests from Deck 11 to proceed to disembarkation. Please make sure you have all of your belongings with you. We thank you for sailing with us and wish you a safe onward journey."

Samatha and Sean joined the calm procession of passengers making their way to the gangway. The air was filled with polite chatter and the soft clatter of rolling suitcases. Once inside the cruise terminal building, they reached the luggage hall where suitcases were neatly arranged in color-coded groups under large signs indicating cabin decks.

"There we are—Deck 11," Sean said, pointing to a tidy row of suitcases resting against a backdrop of the number **11** taped to the wall.

Samatha spotted her bags quickly. "These two are mine," she said, tugging at one of the handles.

"Let me help," Sean offered, stepping forward and lifting both bags with ease onto a nearby luggage trolley. "Wouldn't want you pulling a muscle on the last day."

"Thank you, porter Sean," she teased, giving him a playful smile.

Together, they wheeled their trolleys toward the large sliding doors that opened to the outside world. As they stepped out of the terminal building, the brisk morning air greeted them. The sun was out, casting a golden glow over the long-stay car park, and the temperature sat at a chilly but refreshing **7 degrees Celsius**.

Outside, the scene was a mixture of cheerful reunions and logistical hustle. Taxis lined up along the pavement with drivers holding up name cards. Minivans and private cars circled through, pulling up to collect their loved ones. Families greeted returning passengers with open arms, kisses on the cheek, and warm hugs after two weeks apart.

One elderly woman ran into her granddaughter's embrace with tears in her eyes. A man in a business suit shook hands with his teenage son as they loaded bags into the boot of a blue SUV. There was laughter, honking, and the sound of zippers being opened and closed.

Sean turned to Samatha, his expression calm but a little hesitant.

"My car's just over there," he nodded toward the long-stay car park across the street. "Would you like a lift? I've got plenty of space in the boot."

Samatha smiled gently, touched by the offer. "That's kind of you, Sean, but no need. My friend is on her way to pick me up. She should be here any minute."

Sean looked slightly disappointed, but he nodded with understanding. "Of course. I just thought… one last leg of the journey together."

Samatha tilted her head, her voice soft. "I'm really glad we met, you know. This cruise… it wouldn't have been the same without you."

He chuckled, trying to mask the emotion behind his grin. "Same here. From karaoke nights to late-night cake at Dickens — definitely made some memories."

They stood for a moment in comfortable silence, both aware that their time together was drawing to a close. Then, from the edge of the crowd, a small silver car pulled up to the pavement, and a woman inside waved at Samatha through the windshield.

"That's her," Samatha said.

Sean helped her load the suitcases into the car's boot, then stepped back.

"Well," he said, brushing his hands together, "Safe journey, Samatha."

"Thank you," she said, and then surprised him with a quick hug. "Take care of yourself, Sean. And don't forget—submit that photo to the next competition."

He laughed. "Only if you're my creative director again."

Just before Samatha stepped into the car, she turned back to Sean one last time.

"Oh! Almost forgot," she said, pulling her phone from her coat pocket. "Let me send you the photos we took. I'll put them all in a WhatsApp album so you have them."

Sean smiled, already reaching for his phone. "Great idea. I was going to ask. I've got a few good ones of you pretending to be a ship's captain."

Samatha laughed. "That one stays between us."

They exchanged numbers quickly and added each other to their contacts. A moment later, her message came through: "Cruise Memories 📷⚓" — with over a dozen photos attached, from wide fjord landscapes and smiling selfies on deck, to blurry shots of late-night shows and their table at the Buckingham restaurant.

"There. That should hold you over until the next cruise," she said with a wink.

Sean gave a thoughtful nod. "We've shared a lot in these two weeks. I'd really like to keep in touch."

"Me too," Samatha replied warmly. "Who knows, maybe we'll end up on the same ship again someday."

He stepped back as her car started to pull away, waving as it joined the line of traffic outside the port. As he stood there in the crisp morning air, phone in hand and suitcase by his side, a quiet smile spread across his face.

With one last wave, Samatha got into the car. The vehicle pulled away slowly, and Sean stood there for a moment, watching it disappear into the morning traffic.

Then, with a small sigh and a fond smile, he turned back toward the long-stay car park, suitcase handle in hand, the memories of the last two weeks already replaying in his mind.

A journey had ended—but perhaps, just perhaps, a new one had begun.

Though the journey was over, the connection they built would sail on—message by message, photo by photo.

Two Solo Together

EPILOGUE

Until We Sail Again

As the final goodbyes were exchanged and the last suitcases rolled away from Tilbury Cruise Terminal, the ship that had once been their floating home slowly faded into the background. What remained were the memories—rich, vivid, and stitched together by laughter, new experiences, and companionship.

Samatha sat quietly in the back seat of her friend's car, scrolling through the photo album she had just sent Sean on WhatsApp. There were silly moments, awe-inspiring views, snapshots of meals that looked almost too pretty to eat, and impromptu selfies with wind-tousled hair and genuine smiles. It had only been two weeks, but the bond she and Sean had formed felt timeless.

Meanwhile, Sean drove through the long-stay car park exit, glancing at his phone during a red light. A new message pinged in from Samatha: **"Already missing sea days... and you."**

He smiled, typing back:
"Next time, same cabin deck?"
"Deal. ☺"

Some people come into your life for a brief moment, yet leave behind a permanent mark. For Sean and Samatha, a solo cruise became something much more: a chapter of youth rekindled, friendship rediscovered, and the quiet promise of more stories to come—whether on land or at sea.

The End... or just the beginning

"**Two Solo Together**" is a heartwarming travel tale of unexpected friendship, shared adventures, and the quiet magic of life at sea.

When Samatha and Sean board a solo cruise from London Tilbury, neither expects much more than scenic views and buffet dinners. But two weeks, nine ports, and countless laughs later, their journey becomes far more than a holiday—it becomes a voyage of rediscovery. From the charming streets of Bergen to formal dinners, talent shows, sea day surprises, and unforgettable performances at the Palladium, their bond deepens with each passing day.

Through gentle humour, vivid travel moments, and warm connections, *Two Solo Together* captures the joy of finding kindred spirits when you least expect it. A story about friendship, renewal, and the lasting memories made far from home.

J. Darby

" **Two Solo Together**" is a tender tale of two solo travellers brought together by chance—and held together by something deeper.

When Samatha and Sean embark on a cruise from London Tilbury, both are content to journey alone, hoping only for some peace, fresh scenery, and maybe a friendly conversation or two. But from the first shared breakfast to late-night shows, mountaintop views in Norway to quiet moments in lounges and laughter under soft lights, their connection grows with every tide.

As the ship sails through changing skies and foreign ports, so too do their hearts navigate unfamiliar but thrilling waters. In two unforgettable weeks, what begins as companionship slowly becomes something more. But when the journey ends, will their story?

Two Solo Together is a gently romantic, feel-good voyage of unexpected connection, soulful moments, and the kind of love that arrives softly— but stays.

S.M. Paul

" **Two Solo Together**" is a story of timing, fate, and the kind of connection that sneaks up on you in the most unexpected of places.

When Samatha boards the cruise ship at London Tilbury, she's not looking for love—just a break from routine, and maybe a view worth photographing. Sean, quiet and observant, has his own reasons for sailing solo. Neither expects much from the journey—until a fateful breakfast brings them together.

Through windswept decks, laughter-soaked dinners, and stolen moments in hidden lounges, a spark begins to flicker. But as the ship approaches its final port, questions linger. Was it just a holiday romance... or the beginning of something real?

Set against the majestic backdrops of Norway's fjords and the sea's shifting moods, Two *Solo Together* is a heartfelt tale of rediscovery, second chances, and the powerful tides of human connection.

Y. P. Matyn

Two solo travellers. One cruise ship. Zero plans to fall for each other.

Samatha was ready for some "me time." Photography, pastries, and peace. Sean just wanted to avoid cruise karaoke. Neither expected their solo cabins would lead to shared breakfasts, onboard mischief, and far too much champagne.

From guessing whodunnit in wild theatre shows to dodging overpriced laundry services and hiking up Norwegian mountains in questionable weather, these two manage to turn every sea day into a small adventure—and every quiet moment into something a little magical.

Packed with travel mishaps, cheeky banter, cruise ship charm, and a slow-burn friendship that may just set sail into something deeper—Two *Solo Together* is the perfect feel-good read for anyone who knows love doesn't always arrive on schedule… but sometimes finds you anyway.

A.L. Morgan

A Cruise. A Chance Encounter. A Journey Neither Will Forget.

When Samatha boards a two-week Nordic cruise, she's armed with a camera, a suitcase full of cosy jumpers, and zero expectations beyond scenic ports and peaceful mornings. Across the solo traveller's table sits Sean—easygoing, curious, and just as surprised to be making a new friend at sea.

From lazy sea days with breakfast in bed to windswept hikes in Bergen, champagne-fuelled lunches, and evening shows full of laughter and intrigue, what begins as casual companionship soon blossoms into something far deeper.

But as the final port looms and their journey nears its end, Samatha and Sean must face the question every shipboard romance eventually asks: is it just the magic of the sea… or something real enough to carry home?

Set against the breathtaking fjords of Norway and filled with quirky cruise traditions, heartfelt moments, and the quiet thrill of unexpected connection, Two *Solo Together* is a heartwarming tale of friendship, timing, and the adventure of letting someone in.

B. S Lincey

"Two strangers. One cruise. A voyage that changes everything"

"Love doesn't follow the itinerary."

"They boarded alone—but the sea had other plans."

"A Nordic escape. An unexpected connection. A story written in waves."

"When you stop searching, you just might find the heart you've been missing."

"She packed a raincoat, a camera—and accidentally found a man."

"He came for the buffet. She came for the fjords. Love came unannounced."

"One cabin, countless laughs, zero regrets."

"Sometimes the best part of the cruise... isn't the destination."

ABOUT THE AUTHOUR
Dr. Kesorn Pechrach Weaver

Kesorn is a highly multiple skills include engineering, entrepreneur, business and research scientist with international research, collaboration with research organisations and bring products to the market. Her background experience is sensors, industry, medical devices, pharmaceutical, DNA, microfluidic, mental health, cells, Biomarker, smart material, semiconductor, agricultural engineering, smart city and introduce new products. Her skills include experiments, testing, simulation, prototypes, designed electrical system, business, management, intellectual property (IPR) and commercial exploitation.

PECHRACH PUBLISHING

All books under this author are available to order fromfrom bookshops and online platform.

1. Arc Control in Circuit Breakers: Low Contact Velocity, 2nd, ISBN 978-0-9931178-7-9

2. Piezoelectric in Prosthetics:Energy Harvesting, ISBN 978-0-9931178-2-4

3. Born from Kidney Transplant Mother, ISBN 978-0-9931178-4-8

4. Civil Servants Salary in Thailand, ISBN 978-0-9931178-5-5

5. Slow Contact Opening Circuit Breakers, ISBN 978-0-9931178-6-2

6. Architecture Technology for Engineers, ISBN 978-0-9931178-3-1

7. Piezoelectric in Circuit Breakers, ISBN 978-0-9931178-0-0

8. 37 Smart Ways: Life Journeys, ISBN978-0-9931178-1-7

9. Arc Control in Circuit Breakers, ISBN: 978-3-6392210-1-5

10. When my Son become Novice Monk in United Kingdom, 2018, ISBN: 978-0-9931178-8-6

11. When my Son become Novice Monk in United Kingdom, edition 2, 2018, ISBN: 978-0-9931178-9-3

12. Evaluation Horizon European Feasibility, 2018, ISBN: 978-1-912957-00-2

13. Evaluation Horizon European Innovation, 2018, ISBN: 978-1-912957-01-9

14. Arts and Artists Buddhapadipa London, UK, 2019, SBN: 978-1-912957-02-6

15. Proposal Horizon European Research and Innovation, 2019, ISBN: 978-1-912957-03-3

16. Arduino App Bluetooth Robotics, 2019, ISBN-13: 978-1912957-06-4

17. Create Educational Robotics, 2019, ISBN-13: 978-1912957-04-0

18. Robotics Class, 2019, ISBN-13: 978-1912957-05-7

19. Graphene Materials Engineering Architecture, ISBN-13 : 978-1912957-09-5

20. Two Solo Together, ISBN-13 : 978-1912957-10-1